TRAPPED WITH THE DUKE

ANNABELLE ANDERS

ANNABELLE
ANDERS

Trapped With The Duke

Copyright © 2021 Annabelle Anders

Cover Art by Forever After Romance Designs

MISS JONES' NEW POSITION

"*I*'m not at all happy having this Miss Jones person at your establishment, Miss Primm."

Collette Jones, the new language teacher at the esteemed seminary for ladies, paused in the corridor when she overheard herself being discussed inside of her employer's office. The complaining voice belonged to a particularly vocal parent, Mrs. Metcalf and, quite frankly, the woman's sentiments came as no surprise.

Even if the speed at which she disclosed them was somewhat concerning.

Not quite ten minutes earlier, the woman had interrogated Collette in her classroom. "*You are one of Lord Chaswick's... sisters, then?*" The woman's brows had risen so high, they'd nearly disappeared in her hair.

And by sisters, it was obvious she meant *illegitimate* relations. Because Collette's mother had not been married to Lord Chaswick's father. The news of their connection had only been made public last spring.

"Miss Jones has outstanding qualifications and will fit in

quite well," said Miss Primm, her tone carrying an air of finality. "In fact, we're thrilled to have a teacher as passionate about Latin and French as she is. Your daughters stand only to benefit from Miss Jones' instruction."

"She is a proper lady, despite her birth," another voice added. That would be Miss Shipley coming to her defense, Miss Primm's assistant headmistress.

"That remains to be seen," Mrs. Metcalf responded. "But take note that I do *not* approve of a bastard teaching my little darlings. They are quite impressionable, you know."

Collette rolled her eyes heavenward. Did the woman think the circumstances of her birth were catching? Hearing Mrs. Metcalf speak thusly, she struggled to understand the idiosyncrasies of society.

Which was precisely why she'd chosen to teach, rather than allow her brother and sister-in-law to introduce her to one bachelor after another.

"We are sufficiently confident in her abilities," Miss Primm stated matter-of-factly.

"Well, I don't know..."

The Metcalfe girls—Prudence, Patience, and Charity—were ages twelve, fourteen, and sixteen, respectively. This was to be their first semester attending Miss Primm's Private Seminary for the Refinement and Education of Ladies.

Emphasis on *Refinement*.

All of the students were returning from summer holiday today and the week would mark Collette's first as a teacher.

"You'll see. Come the end of term, you'll be as happy as we are that Miss Jones has joined our staff. Were you aware that her younger sister recently married the Marquess of Greystone?" The ever-proper Miss Shipley, of course, would be well aware that Collette's connection to a lofty title would be more persuasive than her actual teaching abilities.

"A travesty." Mrs. Metcalfe announced. "What is the world coming to?"

Shaking her head, and thinking the conversation must be nearing its conclusion, Collette backed away from Miss Primm's office and all but ran to her classroom.

My classroom! A place where she would teach *her* lessons, to *her* very own students.

Stepping inside, her gaze flew to the board where she'd written her name in perfect script. *Miss Jones.*

Simply because she'd been born on the wrong side of the blanket didn't mean she hadn't been properly educated. Her brother—her half-brother, to be more accurate—was a wealthy baron and had provided Collette and her younger sisters with excellent governesses from the moment he'd discovered their existence. And after he'd married last spring, he'd offered her the choice to either enter society or pursue her career in teaching.

Her decision had been an easy one.

Unwilling to subject herself to the censure of the *ton*, Collette had chosen teaching. It was all she'd ever hoped for, and now, at the age of two and twenty, her dream was coming to fruition.

She simply needed to get through her first day, and then her first week.

And then the next one.

Collette strode to her desk and went to work organizing her affects for the umpteenth time that morning, and yet, still, she couldn't keep her hands from shaking.

Dratted nerves.

Because, truth be told, she never would have been offered the position if not for a considerable donation made by her brother—in exchange for one small favor.

"Pardon me," a cultured voice said from the open door.

Collette glanced up to see who was interrupting her last few moments of solitude and immediately straightened. Because that was what one did when in the presence of a duke.

He cocked one distinguished brow. "Have you seen a young miss, about so high? Blond hair, brown eyes—?"

"Lady Fiona." She knew exactly who he was referring to and exactly who he was as well. Most of their students came from families on the periphery of the elite. They attended because their parents hoped their daughters' manners and charm would attract a titled and/or wealthy husband.

Lady Fiona had no need of either. Because the man standing before Collette was the girl's older brother, the Duke of Bedwell.

Her first thought was that she certainly mustn't draw any complaints from him.

Her second thought was that he was even more good-looking close up than he had been when one of her fellow teachers, Miss Fortune, had pointed him out to her at the orientation earlier.

Not quite a full foot taller than her own less than imposing height, his elegant dress and demeanor made her feel as though he must be at least ten feet tall. He held a perfectly shaped tall black hat in his hands and not a single strand of his golden-brown hair was out of place. From the tone of his voice, she would have imagined him showing a friendly sort of expression, but his jaw was set, and the eyes directed at her were the coolest blue possible.

4

"Have you seen her?" He sounded annoyed now, and Collette blinked and dropped her gaze back to the papers on her desk. What on earth was she doing? Ogling one of her student's brothers?

Who also happened to be a duke!

"I believe she was leading a group of students upstairs to the sleeping quarters. I overheard an abundance of giggling and footsteps headed for the back stairwell a few moments ago."

Lady Fiona, of course, was very popular. And not simply because of her station in life. Collette had realized that the moment she met her. The girl, just four and ten, was unusually charismatic, good-natured, and kind. And if a few of the other teachers were to be believed, Lady Fiona Brierton was incredibly gifted in mathematics and the sciences.

The duke merely nodded, looking down his nose, and then, perfectly at ease with himself, strode toward the window where he stood silently staring outside.

A man such as he, she presumed, wouldn't think it necessary to make conversation with a teacher or provide her with an explanation for his presence. But thinking it best to stay hidden from Mrs. Metcalf, she simply sat quietly staring at her papers.

She clutched her hands in front of her, wishing she'd listened more to some of her sister-in-law's instructions on all the dos and don'ts for dealing with dukes. No doubt, even her sister Diana would find something clever to say.

"She is a lovely girl, your sister," Collette offered. "I imagine you miss her while she's away."

Collette studied his straight back, noticing the exquisite cut of his clothing, her eyes skimming down the back of a perfectly fitted jacket, tan breaches hugging his thighs, and lower, to where shining Hessians were planted shoulders' distance apart.

"You must be proud of her," she added.

"I'd be prouder if she'd not insisted on attending this plebeian institution." His response startled her.

Plebeian institution? Miss Primm's School attracted young ladies from all over England! Although... Very few of those daughters hailed from ducal families.

In fact, as far as she knew, Lady Fiona was the first.

And only.

Collette stepped away from her desk and extended her right hand. She wasn't one of those simpering debutantes she'd witnessed last spring. She was a teacher. And as a representative of the school, she would make him well aware that although the women at Miss Primm's might be *plebeian*, they were not to be dismissed so easily.

"I am Miss Jones, Your Grace, and I shall be teaching your sister Latin this year." She stood behind him, allowing him no choice but to turn and acknowledge her. "And French."

When he did so, those icy blue eyes flicked to her outstretched hand as though she were offering him a snake. Which didn't quite make sense until she realized her mistake.

She wasn't wearing any gloves.

Indecision swept through her. Perhaps she ought to have curtsied instead.

Too late now.

With raised brows, he reached out and took her bare hand in his gloved one.

Oh, yes. She most definitely ought to have curtsied instead.

Because as he clasped her hand in his, she straightaway found herself in a state of total awareness—of his maleness —of his *dukeness.*

The warmth of his soft gloves enclosed around her fingers—fingers that were always cold. And before she could shake his hand, as she'd intended to do, he bent over and brushed his lips just above her knuckles.

"The Duke of Bedwell, at your service, Miss Jones."

Unfortunately, for both of them—but mostly for her— her response to his formal greeting was an almost-snort and then a gurgling sound that she quickly smothered. The Duke of Bedwell had kissed her *bare hand*!

She'd had her hand kissed before, but only by a few of her brother's closest friends, and she'd *always* been wearing gloves. Perhaps she ought to have risked another encounter with Mrs. Metcalf after all.

She cleared her throat. "I hope we can disabuse you of your prejudice."

The duke raised his brows.

"Against the school—your prejudice against the school."

"I have nothing against the school, Miss Jones. Not for other students, anyhow. But this is not the proper place for my sister to be educated. I'm only allowing her to attend because she is adamant about doing so. She would be better off learning at home, from a private governess and various tutors."

That would leave the very sociable young lady with only adults for company. Lady Fiona would be miserable.

"If she were to do as you wish, she would miss out on friendships and the satisfaction that comes from learning with others. We have concerts, games, and outings…"

"Are you really so keen on arguing with me today, Miss

Jones? On your first day, if I am not mistaken?" How did he manage to appear so dashing while acting so disagreeably?

However, his words had her clamping her mouth closed.

"You are not mistaken." She could not afford another complaint. Especially not if it came from the Duke of Bedwell. "And no, I am not. Well, not that I wish to argue with you on any other day, either. I only wished to reassure you…"

There was no mistaking the exasperation in his gaze this time.

"I'm so very sorry, Your Grace." *Stop talking Collette.* "It goes without saying that you know what's best for Lady Fiona." *Except, you don't really.* But she held her tongue this time.

He glanced toward the door. "What is taking my sister so long? Surely, she's not unpacking her trunks?"

"Oh, no. Likely she's excited to meet new friends. I've no doubt they'll be down shortly." She glanced out the window. "Any minute now, in fact. Everyone is already leaving for the park. The girls won't want to miss any of the Welcome Tea festivities."

The students, teachers, and parents alike traditionally celebrated the launch of a new school year with Miss Primm's Welcome Tea in the park in the center of town. Although, from the descriptions she'd heard, it sounded like more of a picnic than a formal tea, what with the games, contests, and a small ceremony.

Already, most of the students had exited the school to stroll along the dirt road while many of their parents rode in fine carriages to the venue. The cook and maids and all sorts of offerings had been driven over earlier so that they could set up the chairs and have all the preparations in place for their guests.

Collette, too, ought to be making her way to the tea. As a teacher, she would be expected to assist in serving. If she left quickly and ran part of the way, she just might be able to arrive in time. She bit her lip and moved toward the door.

"You are welcome to go up and fetch her yourself, Your Grace. You know how young girls are, most likely they're so busy talking that they've forgotten the time. If you'll excuse me..."

"Miss Jones." His voice prevented her escape. "I'm unfamiliar with the layout of the school, and I hardly think it proper for a gentleman to wander alone in the young ladies' private quarters."

"Oh... yes." He was right, of course. Collette could simply fetch Lady Fiona herself.

However... perhaps he'd feel better about leaving his sister here if he saw how clean and orderly the dormitory had been set up. And she knew for a fact that Lady Fiona had been allotted one of the newer beds and that her desk was near the window that offered the very best view.

"I'll show you upstairs, if you'd like, Your Grace." That way, after the duke had returned home, he could imagine his sister hard at work at their lovely school rather than worry that he'd made a mistake sending her here.

He pursed his lips.

"Very well."

Collette exhaled. "Right this way."

~

ONLY AFTER MISS JONES had turned to lead the way did Addison stretch his shoulders. He was more than half tempted to have Fiona collect her belongings and return home with him at once.

If not for the fact that his mother had sided against him on this, despite admitting to having reservations regarding the Chaswick Scandal, he never would have allowed it.

But his mother rarely denied Fiona anything her heart desired. Which meant he rarely did either.

No, his reluctance had had nothing to do with one of Chaswick's illegitimate sisters teaching Fiona. It would have been hypocritical if it had.

Rather, such a school was not the proper place for the daughter of a duke. The duties she stood to face as an adult differed greatly from anything her fellow students would ever understand. His sister was different. Just as he was. They could not dismiss the responsibilities that came along with their position.

Allowing Miss Jones to lead him, he noted a display made up of colored flowers along with cutout letters pinned together welcoming students back.

Miss Primm's Private Seminary for the Education of Ladies was decent enough, but in the brief time since he'd arrived, he'd been harangued by no less than half a dozen social-climbing mothers.

If the mothers were already attempting to elevate themselves through him, how many of their daughters would befriend his unsuspecting sister for the very same reason?

"There are two stairwells; this one isn't nearly as impressive, but it is the closest," Miss Jones glanced over her shoulder as she fumbled with a latch. "This shouldn't be locked," she mumbled before jerking the door open.

Filtered sunshine from a window high above provided just enough illumination for him to know that he'd have much preferred to utilize the larger staircase—one that was more than spiraling steps winding up a space that qualified as little more than a closet.

He set his jaw and inhaled a deep and calming breath. Chalk dust, lemon oil, and some other scent that was only ever present in schools assaulted his olfactory sense. Except for a hint of something sweet—the same scent he'd caught a whiff of when he'd kissed her hand.

He certainly hoped Miss Jones was more proficient at languages than she was at propriety. Offering her hand to him as though she were a gentleman intent upon sealing a contract. And no gloves!

The back of her wrist had felt cool when he'd brushed his lips over her skin. She'd smelled like chalk dust but also something sweet.

Vanilla? Mint?

He clasped the rail of the spiral staircase and glanced up to find her derriere directly in his line of sight. Nothing spectacular about it, really. She was petite and thin but not quite bird-like. Even so, he didn't immediately drag his gaze away.

"The older girls' dormitory is on the top floor," she explained as she climbed past the first landing. "The youngest girls are on the same floor as a few of us teachers. Since this is my first-year teaching, I don't rank my own chamber just yet."

Addison forced his attention away from the gray walls to the fabric of her gown fluttering in front of him.

The walls are not closing in on me. He knew this rationally and yet despite being in excellent physical condition, the moment he'd stepped into the stairwell, his chest had tightened. It was ridiculous and yet… it was not.

Grasping at the nearest distraction, he pinned his gaze on the schoolteacher's bum and managed to draw a decent amount of air into his lungs.

He could endure the confinement for the moment. They would be exiting in a matter of seconds.

Her gown was prettier than something he'd imagined a teacher wearing. An eggshell-blue color, and someone had crocheted tiny daisies around the hem. A filtered ray of sunshine from the window overhead caught her blond hair, which might be attractive if she'd not bound it so tightly.

She was of average height and not as frail as most English ladies. Only she wasn't a lady, really. She was Lord Chaswick's illegitimate sister. The scandal had been just significant enough to create a stir for the second half of last spring's season.

Truth be told, Addison rather admired the baron for publicly acknowledging his sisters—even if some members of the *Ton* disapproved. He, himself wouldn't have given it a second thought if his mother hadn't made such a fuss over it.

As Addison slid his hand along the smooth rail, a cold bead of sweat dripped down the back of his neck reminding him again of his fear. He forced his hand to relax. This was only a stairwell. He was in no danger, for God's sake.

From what he'd gleaned before entering, the building was four stories high. He glanced longingly at the door that exited onto the third floor but refused to give in to his incomprehensible weakness.

Miss Jones, however, oblivious to the state of his nerves,

lifted her dress and took each step carefully, not showing herself to be in any sort of hurry.

Her ankles were prettier than he would have expected as well. Shapely.

With only one flight remaining, Addison allowed himself to focus his attention on the swaying movement of her hips, barely discernible beneath that light blue muslin. Her legs would be strong, muscular, no doubt, but slim. When she arrived at the last landing, she dropped her skirts, and he trailed his gaze up to her back, relieved and disappointed at the same time.

But mostly relieved.

Because as much as he'd enjoyed the view climbing these stairs that had been designed, it seemed, to only accommodate small children, the ability to breathe normally held a higher place on his current list of needs.

Addison stepped onto the landing which was barely large enough for the two of them and draped his arm over the balustrade to keep from having to drop it around her.

Thank God.

Only... Perhaps he was thanking his maker too soon.

Miss Jones was frowning and tugging at the door. "What the devil?" She was mumbling beneath her breath again.

Foreboding tightened his chest even more.

"It's locked." She exhaled and then grunted. The ceiling was angled above them, making this particular landing smaller than the ones exiting onto the lower floors. Was it getting even smaller?

"Move aside." Despite his heart pounding in his ears, he checked his impatience as she maneuvered herself around him, unable to avoid his arms brushing against hers. She was all but pressed against his back as he took his turn at the handle and tugged.

The door didn't budge.

And again.

Nothing.

After a few more attempts, he conceded that someone had locked it from the other side.

"It's usually propped open. I can't imagine why it would be locked." She'd apologized at least ten times now in between expressions of dismay as she edged around him again and gave the door one last tug. "Hello out there!" She pounded. "Is anyone there? We're locked in here." Her calls for help echoed loudly and after a moment, Addison became painfully aware that they would go unheeded.

"Nothing to worry about. We can exit on the third floor." Her voice sounded tighter than it had moments before. "If this is some sort of prank, so help me…"

Addison wasn't comprehending much of what she was saying as all his focus was trained on his breathing—or rather his lack thereof. He wiped one hand across his brow.

"Yes. The third floor," he managed to answer despite his lips going numb.

He did not wait for her to descend first. He could not wait. Not if he wished to maintain his dignity.

Taking swift and deliberate steps, Addison all but flew down to that third-floor landing.

Where this door, too, refused to budge.

"I don't understand it!" her voice wailed from behind him as they descended to the second floor, where yet again, and almost not surprisingly by now, they discovered it to be locked as well.

That drop of cold sweat he'd felt earlier had multiplied

into several now, on his brow, his hands… the back of his neck.

He needed to get outside. He needed to see the sky—the sunlight. He needed to breathe fresh air, unconfined by this godforsaken stairwell. Addison skipped every other step on the way to the first floor where they'd entered.

But when he grasped the handle in order to escape to his freedom, black crept around the edges of his vision.

It was locked.

Holy Mother of God, they were trapped.

His knees all but gave out on him as he lowered himself to sit on the bottom step.

THE INCIDENT

*C*ollette stepped past the duke to try the door herself, but something in his demeanor had her turning to study him instead. Even with only the dim light coming through the window at the very top of the stairwell shaft, she could tell that something was wrong.

"Your Grace?"

He'd removed his gloves and was pressing neatly trimmed and buffed fingertips to his forehead. His eyes were closed, and his breath hissed as he seemed to struggle for control.

Was he terribly angry with her? He was a duke, after all, and she'd gotten them trapped in this horrid little stairwell. If she were to judge by his disapproving demeanor in her classroom earlier, he likely was doing his best to keep from strangling her right about now.

But no, he seemed to have forgotten her presence altogether.

Collette lowered herself to her haunches and closer,

noticing his breaths seemed shallow and labored. "Your Grace?" she whispered. "Are you unwell?"

"It's nothing," he barely managed to gasp. "I'm fine..." When he stared at her from those icy-blue eyes of his, the disdain from earlier was noticeably absent. Was that panic?

Was he having apoplexy?

"Get someone to open—" he inhaled sharply "—that blasted door."

Collette nodded and then bit her lip. She'd once gotten herself trapped beneath her bed and thought she was going to die. Fortunately, the feeling had lasted barely thirty seconds as she'd managed to wedge herself out in her panic.

But the duke could not wedge himself out of this stairwell.

And he was, indeed, terribly unnerved.

"Stay right there." She pressed a hand to his knee and then realized the futility of her advice as she pushed herself to her feet and started pounding on the door again. "Help! We're stuck in here! Someone help!"

She paused every half a minute or so, hoping to hear someone answer, and then started up again when none came. The more she pounded in vain, the less fervent her shouts became.

If anyone heard her, they were being exceedingly rude not to come to their aid. She only wished that was the case.

"Everyone must have left for the picnic already." She turned her back to the door and slid downward until her bum landed softly on the floor. He really was quite pale.

She hoped he wouldn't faint, or vomit. Did dukes vomit? She immediately chided herself for being ridiculous. Of course they did.

He was a flesh and blood human, like herself—even if only in regard to the most basic aspects of his person.

A glance at her reddened fists had her contemplating that her voice felt equally raw. She hated feeling helpless. As the oldest of all her sisters, she was a doer—a fixer.

She couldn't just sit here doing nothing! Collette rose, scrambled up the steps, and proceeded to pound and holler on the second, third, and then the fourth floor with the same dismal results.

By the time she returned to where he was sitting, although still pale, he was sitting up straight. If not for the sweat hovering above his lip, she could almost wonder if she'd imagined his anxiety.

"I'm terribly, terribly sorry," she said between breaths.

At an utter loss, Collette scooted across the floor and then took the space on the step beside him. "No one is likely to worry over my absence from the tea—although they won't be happy to have two less helping hands—but surely, your absence will not go unnoticed?"

If she hadn't been sitting beside him, she would have missed the tremor that shook his much larger frame. The staircase was narrow, however, and most of her side pressed up against his.

"Fiona will be glad of it." The words were the first she'd heard from him in nearly half an hour. He exhaled a long, shuddering breath.

Having dealt with her mother more than once when she'd become overset by one thing or another, Collette decided her best course of action was to take his mind off their situation. Someone would come soon. It wasn't as though they were trapped forever.

"Likely, you are right," she agreed. "I have two younger

sisters myself and more than once I've been called the spoil-sport. Do you have any other brothers or sisters?"

She instinctively settled her fingertips on his knee, which was only inches from hers. Touch was another thing that had helped her mother—providing a connection to reason and calm.

Another tremor rolled through him, this one however, less pronounced. "One brother."

"Is he younger than Fiona?"

"He is older than me."

"But…" She frowned. He could not possibly have an older brother if he was the duke. "How does that work exactly?"

"My father did not marry my brother's mother. He is what's known as a bastard."

Of course.

"I quite understand the concept." She withdrew her hands and hugged her arms in front of her. "As a bastard myself."

He slid her a sideways glance. Until that moment, she'd wager all her pin money that she had been completely uninteresting to him. "Bravo to Miss Primm for hiring you."

His unexpected response bolstered her enough to brave his gaze. "She would not have, if not for my brother."

"Baron Chaswick."

He knew. *Everyone knew.* That the entirety of the *Ton* had been privy to her and her sister's circumstances was one of the things Collette had lamented often with Diana.

With her sister, Lady Greystone now, who was now married and living a life very different than the one Collette had chosen. Not that Collette was jealous of Diana for marrying the marquess, but that she was jealous of the *marquess* for having first claim to her sister now.

"A good man." The duke nodded ever so slightly, drawing Collette out of self-pitying thoughts.

Her brother *was* a good man. He was a very good man. Hearing the duke acknowledge that made him seem a little more likable.

Collette reached into her apron and withdrew the small tin she almost always had on hand. "Have a comfit."

He stared down at it suspiciously.

"It won't kill you. It's just a mint."

"I didn't think it was poison."

Collette ignored him and proceeded to open the small container and hand over two of the candies. She normally only allotted herself one a day, but these circumstances were, in fact, dire. "You look rather pale," she added.

"I—thank you." He accepted them and then popped both in his mouth.

"Perhaps you ought to loosen your cravat."

"I'm fine." But when his eyes shot up and around the stairwell, panic crept into them again.

"Don't think about it," she ordered him. "Look at me." Her words successfully drew his gaze, and she willed him to forget about the locked doors. "Chase. Lord Chaswick—my brother. You know him then?"

He nodded slowly. "We've met on more than one occasion." Even in his diminished state, this man spoke in cultured tones, sounding proper and formal.

"He kept me and my sisters a secret until recently. It was his wife who suggested we enter society. As ladies! Can you imagine? Diana—my sister who is two years younger than me—happily went along with the idea.

"I take it you did not?"

"Good Lord, no! I'd rather be a horse up for auction at Tattersalls—that way, at least, my lack of breeding would be out in the open rather than murmured about behind my back." Collette had done her best to pretend she hadn't been bothered by the whispers, but she and Diana had known many of the same ladies who'd smiled at them one moment, then turned to gossip about them in the next. "Knowing I wished to teach, Chase made inquiries with Miss Primm."

"Along with a sizeable donation."

Collette sat up straight. Even if he had the right of it, she did not appreciate the insinuation that she wasn't up to her task. "For your information, I am highly qualified to teach both Latin and French, and some Greek as well."

He had closed his eyes again, thick lashes fanned out above his cheeks. "But of course," he agreed too easily. "And Miss Primm is going to approve of her newest employee locking herself in a stairwell with one of her student's guardians?"

"But I didn't do it on purpose!"

"Of course, you didn't."

"What are you implying?"

"I'm not implying anything."

He tilted his head back and despite his accusation, Collette couldn't stop her gaze from admiring the strong lines that ran along his jaw and throat to disappear beneath the white linen cloth.

"You aren't seriously suggesting I trapped us together intentionally, are you?" She narrowed her eyes at him. "What kind of a person do you—"

"No." His fingers plucked ineffectively at the knot tied in the cravat around his neck. "I'm not really. But it would be nice to have somebody to blame for this debacle." Twin lines appeared between his eyes as he struggled ineffectually with what was beginning to resemble more of a noose.

"You're tightening it. Turn here." Collette pushed his hands away from the strip of linen, and when he obeyed, she went to work on the knot herself.

His face was but a few inches from hers. What she'd thought had been a shadow was actually light brown whiskers, and she itched to brush her fingertips over them to see if they would feel as scratchy as they looked. His breath was minty, from the comfit, but his scent was also woodsy and spicy and more than a little intoxicating.

She required a good deal of willpower to keep herself focused on the knot.

"Bloody thing is strangling me."

"Are all dukes as ill-mannered as you?" The question escaped before she could think better of it.

"Are all first-year teachers as impertinent as you?"

"As I'm the only first-year teacher of my acquaintance, I'm afraid I cannot answer that." She could almost slip her finger beneath the coil that she hoped would loosen the knot. "But if I were to guess, I would say most likely not."

"It was a rhetorical question."

"Whereas mine was not. Aha!" The knot began to relax. She tugged and then drew the fabric through the loop she'd loosened.

"More than likely, most dukes are perceived as being ill-mannered." He surprised her by providing an answer. "Especially when dealing with impertinent teachers."

Collette scoffed even as she contemplated retying the fabric and giving it a not-at-all gentle tug. Instead, she unwound it, exposing his neck and the base of his throat.

Noticing the shadows and smooth skin there, Collette blinked, struck by the intimacy of it.

"That should help." She dropped her hands and leaned away from him, her own throat feeling unusually constricted.

And still, she couldn't keep herself from watching his hands as he rubbed the skin along his jaw and stretched. When his gaze landed on the walls, he closed his eyes and inhaled before opening them to stare at her again. "Tell me more about your sisters."

Collette didn't have to think very hard to find things to tell him about two of her favorite people in the world.

"Diana loves to dance. She's married now and her husband has made arrangements for her to have formal instruction. I should have been surprised, really, that she married the marquess. Even if he is so much older. She's not quite twenty."

"And you are...?"

"Two and twenty. You are considerably older than Fiona. How old are you?"

He chuckled but answered her anyway. "Seven and twenty."

"Do you get on well with your brother? And yes, I realize it's an impertinent question but..." She shrugged. "We could be here for hours. What else are we to discuss?"

His jaw ticked, and his nostrils flared. Oh, drat. She shouldn't have mentioned their circumstances. "Do you see your brother often? Does he resent you? I thought Chase would resent us when we first met but he's been like a guardian angel since our father died."

"Why did he keep you a secret then?" His voice sounded tighter but still refined.

"To protect his mother's sensibilities. She is… somewhat high-strung. Was your brother's existence ever kept secret from you?"

"God, no." But he didn't expand on his answer. Instead, he startled her by bursting off the stair to pound on the door again. Collette jumped and covered her ears.

His blows were loud enough that if anyone was anywhere in the building, they would hear them. "Hello!" he bellowed. "Open up! At once!"

After he'd spent another sixty or so seconds expending his frustrations, he bowed his head and pressed it against the door.

A heavy sadness weighed on Collette's shoulders as she watched him give up. Seeing such a terribly proud human so defeated and vulnerable felt wrong.

The deliberate rise and fall of his shoulders gave away his struggle to maintain control.

Collette jumped when he landed one last blow to the door—this time using his forehead rather than his fist.

"At the risk of sounding impertinent again, Your Grace, bashing your brains against it isn't going to help this situation."

"But it gives me something else to think about."

"Pain?"

"Yes, he groused, but this time, Collette suspected his irritation was directed more at himself than at her.

His fear was more powerful than she'd imagined.

Collette hugged her arms in front of her, contemplating what she could do to help him.

"Are you close to your brother?" She'd use her curiosity to distract him.

"There is no one I esteem more."

Collette felt the same way about Chase, and she knew without a doubt that her brother loved her and her sisters with all of his heart. But a dukedom didn't stand between them.

"Why?"

He turned his head. "Why do I esteem him?"

"Yes."

"He is my older brother. We were raised together—educated together. Why would I not esteem him?" But there was something else he wasn't saying. Collette pondered two brothers: a younger one and an older one. And if the younger loved the older, he likely looked up to him—saw him as a hero, even. Did this duke feel guilty for inheriting his father's title? But she couldn't ask that. Such an observation would be far too impertinent to make.

Even for her.

FEELING GREEN

*A*ddison resisted the urge to claw at his chest. He never should have entered this stairwell. He never should have set foot inside this Godforsaken school. Every time he opened his eyes, the walls seemed a little closer.

"You said you have two sisters. Tell me about the other one." His voice came out gruff—demanding. When he focused on her, he could almost pretend the two of them weren't locked inside... He brushed away a bead of sweat sliding down the side of his face.

"Oh, yes. Sarah. She is the youngest—just turned ten. Her hair is a little darker than mine, and I imagine she's the smartest of the three of us. Chase hired a special tutor for her—one who could teach her to read on her own. And a special dog as well."

"But she should be reading by now." Addison turned his head enough so he could focus on her face. He would not submit to the spinning feeling assaulting him. He imagined a younger version of Miss Jones. One whose behind didn't

TRAPPED WITH THE DUKE

sway in an exasperatingly suggestive manner when she climbed stairs.

"Sarah was born without sight. It's a wonder, since her eyes are quite lovely. She's the only one of us with brown eyes. Like my mother's."

"Chaswick's father sired all three of you?"

"Yes. He was good to us—he loved us. He provided my mother with a lovely townhouse not five minutes' walk from his other one so he could come home to us often. We didn't know Chase until after Father's death. It was a terrible time for all of us, but meeting our brother helped."

Two families! Good God! Addison tried to imagine living under such... complicated circumstances. He didn't disapprove of the man, what with arranged marriages and all, and yet he couldn't approve either.

He closed his eyes, forcing himself to breathe. What would it have been like to have been raised completely unaware of Rowan's existence and then discover his father had kept him hidden away until after his death? The notion was beyond comprehension.

"I have more mints if you'd like. They seemed to have helped before." He opened his eyes again when the most impertinent Miss Jones's voice sounded much closer. With her proximity came a faint scent of vanilla.

Unwilling to peel himself off the door quite yet, he didn't move.

He was unaccustomed to feeling like a fool.

"Here." She took hold of one of his clenched fists and attempted unsuccessfully to open it. Addison couldn't relax if his life depended on it.

They'd been in this stairwell too long.

Shock, however, did the trick when she slipped one of her small mints between his lips.

Was it his imagination or had her fingers lingered longer than was necessary?

He'd concede the mint helped. He'd not hold such brazenness against her, but neither would he thank her.

"You were looking green again," she offered. "It would be quite unpleasant if you were to—"

"Please don't concern yourself with that." He would not discuss his intestinal fortitude with this woman and would have straightened away from the door if he'd been able.

"Quite right, Your Grace." But she was laughing softly at him.

This time, when she touched his fists, he opened his fingers to accept the hard candy. Her skin was soft, her hands efficiently cool but also feminine.

When she went to pull away, he did not allow it.

Her touch had the effect of reassuring him that the walls were not, in fact, closing in around them.

"How will she read—if she is blind?" he asked, closing his eyes.

"Oh! It's the most incredible invention!" She neither commented on his grasp, nor did she attempt to pull her hand away. In fact, she squeezed his fingers back. "It's all very new. Chase has learned of a Frenchman named Monsieur Braille who developed a code for people who cannot see. Rather than use ink, the code is written with raised dots. So Sarah is going to read with her fingertips." She was all but cradling his fist in both hands now. Fanning his fingers out, she proceeded to draw imaginary circles, almost mesmerizing him. "Monsieur Braille is a leatherworker's son. Punching holes in the leather gave him the idea."

All of Addison's attention homed in on the lines she traced softly in his palm. His chest loosened and the light-headed feeling faded enough to where he could open his eyes.

"I apologize—" The feel of her fingertips took over his entire world. "You don't have to..." And yet he did not release her hand.

It had been poor judgment of him to conclude that she was annoying and boring. Not that she hadn't been boring —initially, that was. And she wouldn't be a teacher if she wasn't at least a little annoying.

But he had been ill-mannered with her and there was no excuse for it, her cheekiness notwithstanding.

Although it had been her idea to lead him up this ridiculously cramped stairwell...

She drew a line along the back of his fingers to his wrist, where the cuff of his shirt and jacket ended, and then dragged her fingertip back to the end of his middle finger.

"Her teacher has brought along a specially trained dog and is showing Sarah how to learn to depend on him to find her way around the estate. Sarah has always been able to maneuver around our home, but only inside, never outside. The dog is supposed to be able to guide her."

Listening to her, Addison simply breathed. She was stroking her finger back and forth in tandem with the beating of his heart. By accident?

"Do you have a dog?" she asked, sounding quite practical and matter-of-fact.

It ought not to have surprised him but summoning the

image of Zeus and Hera almost brought a smile to his lips. "Two, actually."

"And you like them," she said as though she'd discovered something quite significant.

"Of course." Over the years, he'd always had a dog for companionship. He'd learned that losing one was more painful than he ever could have imagined, but living with them made life rather tolerable.

"Hunters?"

"I've had Zeus—my border collie—since I was seven and ten, but took in Hera, my two-year-old English foxhound, more recently.

"From the Greek word *Dyeus*… meaning shine or sky— the highest of the Gods. Is he noble?"

"That's the way Zeus sees himself. At least where Hera is concerned." Although Hera was coming into her own.

"Well, you cannot be as horrible as you seemed earlier if you appreciate dogs." The woman did not know her place.

Intent upon sending her a scathingly disapproving glare, he opened his eyes and…

All thoughts of reprimanding her fled.

Because she was standing closer to him than he had realized, and he'd not expected to be so easily trapped in her gaze. Furthermore, a glimmer of hilarity in that gaze teased him.

The only person who ever got away with teasing him was his older brother, and those times were far and few between. Addison was a duke and could not afford to be taken lightly by others. Growing up, his tutor had instilled in him that such behavior was an insult to the title.

Miss Jones' eyes twinkled back at him as the corners of her mouth tilted upward.

Although the hair she had tied into a knot at the back of her head was blond, the thick lashes fringing her sapphire eyes were nearly black. And those lips formed a perfect cupid's bow. They were full and plump, and no proper teacher should be allowed to walk around wearing them. He didn't understand how he hadn't noticed her mouth the second he'd gotten a good look at her.

Perhaps he'd been distracted by the nonsense coming out of it.

Which brought him back to why he was staring down at her to begin with.

"You believed me to be horrible?" And yet, why did it matter what she believed?

Both her eyes and her smile widened. She shrugged. "Perhaps not horrible, but... at the very least, slightly disagreeable."

"How are you doing that?"

"Doing what?"

"Matching your circles to my heartbeat?" Which was slowing and he could barely hear in his ears now.

Her fingertips froze and she lifted her hand toward his face. Addison instinctively drew back until he realized she was answering his question.

"Right here." The tip of her finger tentatively found the pulse at the base of his neck and then settled there. Her touch felt intimate.

Too intimate.

"I didn't do it intentionally. I was just watching it..."

Pink flooded her cheeks.

He'd never felt more trapped in his life. He straightened and inhaled a calming breath.

"Are your brother and his wife residing in the country

presently?" He might very well need this information sometime in the near future.

"No. They are in London. The dowager prefers it there,
but my understanding is that they will withdraw before the
holidays... Why?"

"So that I can discuss our situation with him."

Because there was no way in hell he was going to be
allowed to walk away from their present circumstances
with his bachelorhood intact. She was unmarried and he a
bachelor and the two of them had already been locked alone
for close to an hour.

She, of course, would be utterly ruined. Illegitimate or
not, she had a baron for a brother and deserved the respect
of any proper lady.

And because of him, her reputation would be in tatters.

"Our situation?" Her eyes narrowed, and two lines
etched between them, just above her impertinent nose.

"Of course. Once we're discovered locked together in
here, we'll have no choice but to marry." Addison's honor
demanded he make an offer.

For the umpteenth time, she caught him unawares.
Because rather than address the situation with the sobriety
it demanded, Miss Jones threw her head back and laughed.

OH, MY!

Only after wiping away tears of laughter did Collette realize the duke was quite serious in his very blunt and unromantic suggestion that they marry. He did not appear at all pleased at her response.

"You are not serious." *He could not be!*

"I assure you, Miss Jones. I would not joke about such a serious matter."

Of course, he wouldn't. She wondered what sort of matters he would, in fact, see fit to joke about.

Collette rubbed her hands down her face. He was too outrageous for words.

"It's not as though the two of us have been caught in a scandalous embrace on some ballroom terrace," she said. That, she believed, was how a lady was compromised. No, this was *definitely* not a ball, and she was not a miss on the marriage mart; she was a teacher. "No one need concern themselves over the two of us being accidentally locked together in a stairwell... Oh, drat." The reminder had him squeezing his eyes together even as that most unattractive green pallor ebbed into his complexion.

Anxious to keep his panic away, she handed him another comfit. Rather than pop this one into his mouth, however, he dropped it in his pocket and reached out his hand.

She blinked at it and then realized he wanted her to distract him again by drawing her invisible lines. Collette wrapped her fingers around his wrist, and his head fell forward. A few more inches and he would be resting on her shoulder.

"Dash it all…" His voice came out tight, almost as though he was struggling to breathe.

"I'm sorry," she whispered. "For bringing…" She clamped her lips together and studied the thickness of his hair. And then, without thinking, moved her hands up and threaded her fingers through the strands, slowly massaging his scalp.

From the bottom to the top and then down again.

"Does this help?" she whispered, and he nodded.

Slow circles, moving from his forehead to the back of his neck.

He groaned.

That was a good sign, was it not?

Over his ears and then back into the thick softness of hair that was not really brown but not blond either. By now his forehead was, in fact, resting on her shoulder.

Roaring filled Collette's ears, but she told herself this meant nothing. He was a duke. He was in distress. Furthermore, he'd used the door for this same purpose. Likely, in a moment or two, he would try to smash his brain into it.

All of which did nothing to calm her own heart, which was racing for no reason at all.

For no reason at all, that was, until he turned his head.

Was that his mouth pressed against her neck? And his hands only gripped her waist to balance himself, didn't they?

Collette licked suddenly dry lips.

"Your Grace?" Her voice came out thready and weak. Good heavens, her nerves were rather unsteady as well, now.

His mouth dragged up her neck, around to her jaw. "Oh…" She exhaled a sigh of surprise because it felt so…

Incredible.

Her heartbeat, thundering in her ears, must be echoing loudly up and down the stairwell.

She lowered a hand to his shoulder. She should push him away. Even she knew this was improper.

Yes, she ought to push him away. And she would.

Just one more moment.

Because his shoulder felt thick and solid beneath her palm and his chest was a stone wall of intoxicating masculinity. How could something be terrifying and yet thrilling at the same time?

What was he doing?

He'd been panicking, hadn't he?

His lips trailed over her chin, to the corner of her mouth, and she tilted her head back.

When Collette decided to teach, she'd told her sister she doubted she would ever know what it would be like to be kissed by a gentleman. Diana, however, had scoffed and insisted that of course she would.

And although Collette would normally resent admitting it—she exhaled a fluttery breath—it seemed that in this instance, her sister had been right.

Because this man was going to kiss her.

It didn't matter that he was a duke or that he was practically a stranger to her. All that mattered were the vibrations coursing through her veins—tremors that shot from her chest to her belly to her limbs.

His mouth nipped the corner of hers, teasing it, teasing her.

"Miss Jones?" Minty breath mingled with her own. Was he asking permission?

Collette pressed up onto her toes and closed the distance between them.

At the same time, his arms tightened around her, and she could feel his person all along her front. He was hard—everywhere. Except for his tongue and his searching mouth, which were tender as he explored and tangled with hers. And except for his hair, soft and thick threaded through her fingers.

He is kissing me.

She had best enjoy it, because she was unlikely to ever experience it again.

His proposal, as honorable as it was, was also somewhat maddening. She had not been born to be a duchess. She'd been born to be a secret.

Being a respectable teacher took her beyond her wildest dreams. It was more than she ever could have hoped for.

The thought was a sobering one.

She loosened her grip, dipped her chin, and lowered her hands. His chest rose and fell beneath her palms, his breathing as labored as hers.

If not for the sound of footsteps approaching from the corridor behind the door, she might have begged him to kiss her again.

His chin jerked up. "Someone is coming." He released her abruptly to pound on the door again.

"Hello!"

"Your Grace?" Miss Shipley called from the other side. And then the door shook.

Collette spun around and all but flew up the stairs, stepping lightly so as to make as little sound as possible. As she passed the landing of the third floor, Miss Shipley's voice carried up the shaft, causing Collette to freeze.

Would she really be ruined if she was discovered alone with him? Was society really so very particular and unforgiving? She raised a hand to her chest, frightened at the possibility that he'd give her away.

But why would he? He cannot seriously want to marry someone like her.

"Your Grace. I am so very sorry. I don't know how this could have happened." Collette winced upon hearing the dismay in Miss Shipley's normally cultured voice. "The banister needed repair and Mr. Driver said he would block the stairwell until he could get around to it. All these doors ought to have been locked... No one should have been able to enter. I am so very, very sorry." Collette could not have imagined Miss Shipley sounding so flustered. The woman, raised to marry an earl, but then jilted by the horrid man, addressed all matters with the utmost of dignity. "Are you unwell, Your Grace? Are you injured in any way?"

"Placing a written sign on the door would have been a better course of action, would you not agree? What if there had been a fire and it was students trapped instead of me? Repairs or not, this door must never be locked in the future. In fact, have them removed. Is the structure even safe?"

The duke sounded more like the man who'd barged into

her classroom earlier than the one who'd been kissing her two minutes before.

"No, Your Grace. And we will have Mr. Driver make the repair to the bannister and remove the locks at once. This will not happen again, I give you my word."

Collette hovered, crouching now, as Miss Shipley and the duke exited the stairwell, other ladies' voices now sounding over theirs. Among them, she heard what sounded like Miss Fortune, along with the unmistakable whining voice that belonged to Mrs. Metcalf.

The door closed and Collette waited until she was sure she was alone. Even after they'd drifted away, however, Collette stayed put, stunned. Her time spent in this small stairwell over the past hour with the Duke of Bedwell did not seem real.

And yet, it had been, and she knew without a doubt that she would never forget it. She touched her lips. That had been her first kiss. Was it the only kiss she'd ever know?

But she could not remain here sighing over something the duke had likely already forgotten. She had students to attend to, duties to perform. She couldn't hide in here forever.

The sound of clanking locks below spurred her into motion. She rose and the very instant she reached for the handle to exit to the fourth floor, the door swung open. Mr. Driver glanced at her hand, which hovered in midair.

"I've already unlocked this one." She swept past him in a hurry.

Cool air hit her cheeks as she shuffled purposefully toward the main stairwell.

That had been close.

Too close.

If she was going to enjoy a long teaching career, she best be far more diligent about who she wandered off alone with.

And that sinking feeling inside of her was not regret. It most certainly was not.

It was relief.

HONOR

*A*ddison clenched his fists at his sides as Miss Shipley promised for the umpteenth time that she'd have the entire school inspected beginning that very afternoon.

"I am terribly sorry, Your Grace. It won't happen again. You have my word." The pleasant-looking blonde woman seemed to be regaining her composure. "Are you quite sure you won't stay for the evening. We'd be honored if you would remain as our special guest for dinner?"

The headmistress's assistant was something of an anomaly in this school. As the daughter of a viscount, she ought to be married and reigning over her own home and children rather than dozens of other people's daughters.

"I am certain." He would return to the privacy of his chamber at the inn. "I'll wish my sister goodbye in the morning."

"But of course, Your Grace." Her smile was proper and her countenance precisely as it ought to be.

She could not be more different than Miss Jones, who, after making a hasty escape, weighed heavily on his conscience.

Stepping outside the school's front door and surmising he had an hour of remaining sunlight, Addison chose to walk the mile or so into the nearby village of Warstone Crossing, sending his carriage ahead. On those occasions when he experienced one of his episodes, fresh air was the most effective at resolving any residual feelings of being trapped.

Hell and damnation, he'd kissed her.

The only explanation he could make for himself was that he'd been out of his mind, and there had been something about her that had kept him grounded.

A shudder of shame ran through him as he recalled the utter lack of control and lack of dignity he'd exhibited. His father would be turning in his grave.

A deep breath and he catalogued the early autumn scents of the meadows around him. One would wonder at any sane person who enjoyed the faint scent of manure woven together with fresh green cuttings and the decay of early falling leaves.

It wasn't as alluring as Miss Jones' sweet vanilla scent, but neither was it as troublesome.

He would speak with her in the morning before bidding Fiona goodbye. No doubt, the teacher was certain that fleeing had eliminated the need for him to remedy what had happened.

It had not.

Because even though they had gone undiscovered, pretending it had not happened did not preclude the fact that he, a bachelor, had been alone with an unmarried lady of some gentility for over an hour. Or that he'd kissed her.

By the time he'd arrived at the small inn, he'd examined the situation from several different angles and, most unfortunately, arrived at the same conclusion every time.

He most assuredly had not seen the last of Miss Jones.

～

"I COULD NOT HELP NOTICING, Miss Jones, that you were not on hand when tea service commenced. Your absence left the other teachers shorthanded. Would you care to explain?" Miss Primm stared at Collette over her spectacles with pinched lips.

Collette inhaled. When she'd not been called into the headmistress's office the evening before, she'd lain in bed conjuring a response in the event she was summoned come morning.

And so, ready with her explanation, she took a deep breath and did her best to appear uncomfortable and apologetic. "I... I... Something I ate did not set well with me. Unfortunately, I was quite indisposed for some time. I am very sorry, Miss Primm. I felt horrible to not uphold my duties—especially on such an important day. But there was nothing I could do..." She intentionally allowed her voice to trail off before peeking up at the stern headmistress.

Augusta Primm's steely gray eyes bore into Collette as the woman considered her explanation. Fighting the urge to squirm under such intense regard, Collette forced herself not to look away. Doing that would be a sure way to indicate she was dissembling.

"I simply wondered because, as I'm sure you know by now, Lady Fiona's brother, the Duke of Bedwell, was locked in the back stairwell. It was most unfortunate, and we are lucky he has not terminated his sister's enrollment." Miss Primm tilted her head questioningly. "You did not overhear him calling for assistance?"

Do not waver.

"I did not. Even if I had, indisposed as I was, I could have done nothing to assist him." She winced. It really was an atrocious confession to make, even when one was lying about it.

Miss Primm nodded slowly and then directed her attention to some paperwork. "Well. I don't suppose there was anything you could have done about... *that.* In the future, needless to say, I advise that you avoid whatever it was that made you ill to begin with. If you'd had an actual class to teach, I would have had to make arrangements for a substitute or teach it myself. I quite understand that one can have no control over when one becomes ill, but it is most helpful if my employees have strong constitutions. The classes at this school"—she pinned her gaze on Collette again—"are only canceled under the most dire of circumstances."

Collette nodded and glanced at the clock sitting on the mantel behind her employer. Her first class, introduction to Latin, began in precisely seven minutes.

"You are excused." Collette went to rise as Miss Primm waved her away, "And Miss Jones?"

"Yes?" Collette halted, half-sitting, half-standing as she hovered over the wooden seat.

"Good luck."

One hour and seven minutes later, as her beginning

Latin students flocked to the exit of her precious classroom, Collette realized why Miss Primm had wished her luck. Ten- and eleven-year-old girls did not have quite the same appreciation Collette had for Latin. In fact, most had seemed entirely unconvinced by her impassioned insistence that when one began comprehending Latin, one would begin to see the world differently.

"And that is a gift. Words have stories inside them," she'd implored. "They travel from place to place. When a person comprehends Latin, they hold a secret key that provides them with a better understanding of science, math, history…"

This was the point where Charity Metcalf had suggested that if only the duke had known Latin, he might not have been trapped in the stairwell the day before. And the other students had dissolved into giggles.

Collette felt no small amount of relief in that her next period was set aside for planning. She needed the time to regroup.

Planting her elbows on her desk, she hid her face in her hands.

"It will get better." Chloe Fortune, instructor of all things philosophical as well as dance, was peeking around the door frame. "I was ready to turn tail and run after my first class as well."

The woman's hazel eyes sparkled in encouragement and her brown hair, although pulled back into a tight chignon, still managed to frame her face with delightful curls. Having spent a good deal of time with Chloe, as the other woman insisted Collette call her in private, she'd learned that Miss Fortune was not only a teacher but had attended and then graduated from Miss Primm's nearly a decade ago.

"Promise?" Collette smiled weakly.

"Would I lie to you?" Chloe's eyes widened innocently as she grinned. "Honestly, don't fret too much. I'd better get back to my classroom. I have two of the Metcalf sisters next hour. If anyone deserves commiserating, it's me."

"And you have it." Collette shooed her away. "Don't be late on my account."

She'd had a few brief conversations with some of the other teachers and although she hadn't gotten as well acquainted with them as she had Chloe, she hoped to forge friendships with them as well. Miss Shipley had told Collette, upon her arrival, that they were like a family here. Collette hoped she had not been exaggerating because although Diana was younger than her by two years, Collette already missed her sister's ever-present companionship.

She missed having someone who knew her moods and cared about her thoughts and feelings and provided the ease of companionship one could only find with family.

Unexpected tears had her wiping at her eyes.

If Diana had been here, Collette could have told her about the kiss. She could have admitted to her that she was quite certain that even when she was old and gray, she would look back on those moments she'd spent in a duke's arms as perhaps one of the great highlights of her life.

She felt her cheeks flush just from thinking about it now.

Collette slipped her tin of comfits out from one of the large pockets sewn into her gown and popped a mint in her mouth. The flavor reminded her of him.

She had *tasted* him!

The Duke of Bedwell had tasted spicy and warm and earthy all at the same time.

Knocking sounds had her hastily tucking the tin away, thinking Chloe might have returned to impart additional words of wisdom. But it was not her friend returning.

Almost as though she'd summoned him with her memory, he was here.

THE BOG

*A*lthough unsmiling, the duke didn't seem quite as intimidating as the last time he'd stepped into her classroom. But of course, that might only be because she'd witnessed him in a weak moment. Even if he had maintained his dignity.

For the most part.

Leaning against the doorframe, he stared at her with raised brows, dangling the same hat he'd had with him the day before on the tip of his glove-covered fingers. His cravat was tied in an elaborate knot, his jacket and waistcoat were pressed, his breeches fit perfectly, and not a hair of his golden-brown hair was out of place.

Hair she distinctly remembered was soft and thick and resisted laying down after one's hands had been running through it.

Had she actually assisted him in removing his cravat less than twenty-four hours ago? It didn't quite seem possible.

"Your Grace." She rose to greet him formally and

brushed a few wayward strands of hair behind her ears. "I did not expect…"

Why was he here?

Curses on the warmth spreading up her neck. And double curses for the tingling she felt all over.

"Miss Jones." He pushed away from the door and glanced over his shoulder. "Miss Primm informed me that you would be free of any obligations presently. Might I request a moment of your time?"

"Of course. Come in. You look much better than the last time I saw you. Not nearly as green." It was true and saying that kept her from mentioning anything embarrassing about her own behavior in the stairwell.

He stared back at her and blinked. "I've been told green is a flattering color on me." Not even a twitch of his lips but… Was he making a joke?

It was her turn to stare at him in surprise. But he spoke again before she could be certain.

"Miss Jones. My actions in the stairwell yesterday were unforgivable. Please allow me to apologize for… my behavior. I've come to—"

"Your Grace, there's no need—you couldn't help it. Were you trapped in a trunk or under a bed or something when you were younger? Or some other tight space?" She'd wondered about his fear while lying awake the night before… when she wasn't thinking about the kiss.

"A bog," he said. And clamped his lips together. "But that's not why I am here—"

"A bog?" She'd heard of such but having been raised in the city, had never actually *seen* one. She half believed they were a terror made up for fairy tales. Ignoring his disgruntled expression, she leaned forward. "As in a muddy hole?"

"Yes."

But a bog was outdoors. "How did you come to fear enclosed spaces after being stuck in mud? Did it cover your face?"

"Came up to here." The duke indicated a line just below his neck. "It was about as deep as they get. But since I was barely six at the time, I found it rather... harrowing. But that is not why I'm here, Miss Jones, I returned this morning to—"

"And no one was there to pull you out? To rescue you?"

"No one knew of my predicament for quite some time. It was long ago, however—"

"How long?"

"About twenty years. Could you possibly allow me to complete a sentence without interrupting me?"

"Not how long ago. I mean how long were you trapped in the bog?" Often, with Chase, she needed to simply plough forward if she wanted her questions answered.

He narrowed his eyes but exhaled what she hoped was a sigh of resignation. "You aren't going to let go of this, are you?"

"Not likely. I've never seen an actual bog and now that you've set my mind to conjuring one, I find myself needing to understand precisely how they work. Are they common? Ought I to warn my sister? Rural living is new to her."

"Sarah? The blind one?"

"Yes."

"You are telling me you grew up in England and have never seen a bog?"

"My sisters and I grew up in *London* and last I heard, there are no known bogs lurking beneath the lawns of Hyde Park."

Another breath and two thoughtful lines appeared between his eyes. "They *can* be dangerous under certain circumstances but are usually nothing more than a messy inconvenience. I'm certain your sister's governess will keep her from meeting with harm."

"But what if she doesn't?"

"Chaswick would not have hired an incompetent woman to care for your sister in the country. Unless the woman is a halfwit, she will know."

Collette chose to ignore the insult that she doubted he realized he'd dealt. Because although she'd never encountered a bog, she was no halfwit.

But... "Could a dog get trapped in one?"

The duke glanced out the window and clasped his hands behind his back. "I've heard stories of an entire ox being swallowed by one."

"Well, that is not at all reassuring."

He turned and rolled his eyes toward the ceiling. "Perhaps, then, you ought to write to your sister and her governess to warn them yourself."

Collette nodded, withdrawing a blank sheet of parchment intent on jotting down the most pertinent information. "An excellent idea. What would you suggest I tell them? In case her governess is ignorant—of bogs—that is."

"They should ask the locals where they are likely to be." He pointed at her paper, apparently resigned to this conversation now. "Bogs are more likely to form in lowlands, and more so after a wet summer, or plentiful rains but not always. And they aren't visible, they appear as normal grasslands but have transformed into what can mostly be described as something of a giant sponge. Most are only a few feet deep—"

"Excepting the ones that eat cattle."

"Excepting those." The duke rubbed his chin. "Best to remind your sister and her governess to stay to the roads until they are familiar with the land. Even then..."

"The bog you were trapped in—was it near your home?"

"It was. I'd been instructed, of course, in no uncertain terms to avoid the west valley. But my brother, Rowan, and a few of the local lads had run off in that direction." Melancholy flickered in his expression before he banked his emotions again.

"And you couldn't help but follow them."

"Precisely." He turned to stare out the window.

Collette tilted her head, guessing at the details he'd not disclosed to her.

He would have followed the group of boys because he loved his older brother and wanted to be included. Did Rowan feel the same toward his younger sibling or did he resent him for usurping him as the heir?

"When I began sinking, I ought to have turned back. But the mud seemed to only be a few inches deep."

Collette folded her hands beneath her chin, picturing him as a small boy. She had no doubt that he would have been quite beautiful. As a duke's heir, he would have been dressed in tailored little breeches and his shoes would always be shined. His hair had likely been lighter then, possibly almost white, and those magnificent icy eyes would have been large in his face, inquisitive and...

He would have been a proud and stubborn child.

"But you did not turn back," she interjected.

After a quick glance around the empty classroom, he pointed to a nearby chair. "Do you mind?"

"Not at all. This is all quite helpful." She dipped her pen

51

into her ink but wasn't really writing any of this down, she would do that later. "You very well might be saving my sister's life by assisting me." *And you are feeding my curiosity.* "Do continue."

"If a person finds themself on unstable ground, it's imperative that they turn back rather than assume it to be passable."

"What did you do?"

He winced, shaking his head. "I ran faster. Which only managed to take me deeper into the bog, putting more space between myself and safety."

"And from help," she added. "Did anyone know where you were going?"

"Much to my regret, no. At first, sinking was a simple annoyance, something to slow my progress. By the time I realized I was in danger of getting caught, I was—"

"Caught," she finished with him.

"Up to my waist." Seated now, he seemed slightly more relaxed than while he'd been standing.

"You couldn't get out."

"Much to my chagrin. And instead of remaining still and calm, as I ought to have, I struggled against it. By the time I was too tired to move anymore, I could barely keep my arms out. And darkness was falling."

The picture he painted was a terrifying one. She hadn't realized that her hand had come up to cover her mouth until she spoke. "Tell me someone found you before nightfall."

"My whereabouts went undiscovered until nearly noon the next day. And by then, I do believe I more resembled a wild animal than the boy they had been searching for." His expression closed off again.

"I cannot begin to imagine what you went through. Nor will I try. Were you injured?"

"A few bruises and various bug bites. Nothing a week confined to my bed couldn't cure."

"Except for the memory."

"Except for the memory," he agreed.

~

USUALLY THE MERE mention of the bog was enough to ruin Addison's mood for at least a week. How many times had he wished this damn memory to perdition? A hundred? A thousand? More?

He hadn't discussed it with anyone for years. In fact, it was so long ago that he only remembered pieces of it.

But Miss Jones had dipped her quill in a bottle of ink and wished to provide helpful information to her sister's governess. He could not fault her for grilling him, especially not when she was doing so out of worry for her younger sister who was blind and living in the country now.

"You mentioned that you should have kept calm and still, but if you did that, how would that have helped your escape?"

"Movement causes the bog—the slurry mixture of mud and water and vegetation—to loosen, which causes a person to sink deeper. Unfortunately, by the time they stop moving, it thickens again, trapping them."

"You have studied this?"

Of course, he had. He'd believed that if he understood it, he could overcome his fears. But the fear persisted. As did the occasional nightmare.

"So how can a person escape?" It seemed he had no choice but to instruct her on all matters bog-related.

"By making small movements with your legs, gradually loosening the material around them until it's fluid enough to pull yourself out."

"And this really works?"

Really? Addison raised his brows. Would he be telling her any of this if it did not?

She tilted her head. "I wonder if we ought to have a lesson on this for our girls. One can never be too careful..."

Having provided her with the necessary information to send to her sister, there were other matters to discuss. "Enough."

She straightened at his tone, as most people did.

Most people, however, did not make him feel guilty for it. Addison clenched his fists and dismissed the smidgeon of remorse threatening at her obvious disappointment.

He'd provided her with enough instruction to keep her students, as well as both her sisters, from getting themselves trapped if they were to stumble upon—God help him —a bog.

However, none of this had anything to do with why he'd needed to meet with her this morning.

She paused, hovering her pen over her piece of paper, and blinked startling blue eyes up at him, and his mind went temporarily blank. What the devil *had* he needed to speak with her about?

She licked her lips and, for no reason at all, his heart skipped a beat. Ah, yes. He remembered.

"Miss Jones." He paused, expecting her to interrupt him with another irrelevant question, and was instead inexplicably annoyed when she set her quill down and folded her hands patiently.

"Miss Jones," he repeated.

"Yes, Your Grace?" Gaze unwavering, she was suddenly all ears, prepared to finally listen to him. Only it wasn't her ears that held his attention, but her mouth, which an irrational part of himself would not be averse to exploring again.

He cleared his throat, "I have come to renew my proposal."

"Your...?"

"We must marry."

Her brows shot up, and she opened her mouth and then closed it again. "But that is not at all necessary. No one but you and I know—"

"That you were trapped in that stairway with me yesterday? For all of an hour? Alone?"

"With no one the wiser, it might as well not have happened." Her eyes flicked to the door with a flinch, and she rose and dashed across the room to pull it closed. Leaning against it, she stared at him. "If you don't mind, Your Grace, I prefer we keep it that way."

"I realize this."

Crossing back to the desk, her apron-covered gown hinted at the delicate hourglass shape of her curves. When she didn't take her seat right away, Addison was obliged to rise as well.

"So, you see—"

"I compromised you yesterday." The fact was irrefutable. "Honor compels me to do the right thing. Honor compels me to marry you."

"It might compel you, but that doesn't mean I will be

compelled as well. The *right thing*, Your Grace, is to leave matters as they are. I finally have the opportunity to be my own person—to be a teacher! My future is... settled!" She was wringing her hands and shaking her head and, for the first time, Miss Jones appeared flustered. "I cannot—I will not—!"

Odd that it would be a marriage proposal that would beckon such panic.

Surely, she didn't intend to refuse him a second time?

"And you cannot want this either," she went on. "I thought I made myself clear yesterday, regarding the nature of my standing. My father was married to another woman, to the baroness, *all while he made a family with my mother.* Regardless of what my brother or sister-in-law do or say, half of society will never acknowledge me. To be perfectly honest with you, I barely fit in here!"

But he was quite aware of her history. "None of that matters." The only thing that mattered was honor. It was everything to him. He'd taken advantage of her.

"Oh, but it does. I beg of you, please, leave matters as they are. You were right yesterday when you said my brother purchased my position here. But even so, Miss Primm willingly hired me. If I was to be involved in a scandal of my own, I would live up to all those nasty things that have ever been said about me. And worse than that, I would disappoint everyone who's ever placed any faith in me."

She was twisting her hands in front of her almost frantically now, not looking torn or even reluctant as she refused his offer.

Fascinating.

It would appear that Miss Jones was a woman who had

no interest in elevating her status through him or any other man. She wasn't wavering in the slightest.

"I kissed you," he reminded her.

At this, her eyes flitted around the room as though it was she, this time, searching for some means of escape.

The kiss had been quite memorable. Was that because of the state he'd been in or because of the woman herself?

And was he willing to press his suit in order to find out?

"It was nothing." She swung her gaze back to him, straightening her back. "Please. Do not mention it to anyone. *I beg of you.*"

And now, she was irritating him again. Was it because of her adamant disinclination to marry him or because she was thwarting his need to act honorably?

Or was it because she had just declared a kiss *that he remembered as distinctly significant* to be nothing?

"So you go about kissing gentlemen that you've only just met often?"

"No! I mean, it was my first, and you were... upset and I was..."

"You were...?"

"I was... there."

"So you think that if I was locked in that room with... Miss Primm, or Mrs. Metcalf, I would have kissed either of them? You think I go about randomly kissing impertinent teachers?"

Addison placed his hat on the surface of her desk and stepped around it, closer to where Miss Jones was standing.

"Well, perhaps not Mrs. Metcalf." Her mouth tightened and he wondered if she wasn't biting back a smile.

"I liked it," he admitted. Why was he arguing the matter? He rubbed his fingers along the tips of his thumbs at his side, keeping himself from… what? Reaching out to see if her hands were as cold today as they had been yesterday? And what would he do if they were?

Warm them?

"That's neither here nor there." The catch in her voice charged the air.

"You liked it too." Addison halted, leaving barely two feet between them.

"I did." She stared up at him. He was satisfied to see that on this matter, she was at least partially torn. "It was… pleasant."

Pleasant?

What the devil? He gave into temptation and took one of her hands in his, noting the rise and fall of her chest and a pink warmth flooding her neck and cheeks. He was not mistaken, then. Pleasant was not an accurate description of how she remembered that kiss.

"Allow me—"

She jerked her hand out of his and stepped back, effectively cutting him off.

"I am sorry, Your Grace. But I have no wish to marry you." She stared straight ahead at what he guessed to be the top button of his waistcoat. "I appreciate your concern, but I give you leave to return to your ducal life knowing that you have done that which is honorable by me. But please… I beg of you to keep this to yourself."

Addison clenched his jaw, unused to the warring responses inside him.

Because his pride was feeling injured by her adamant refusal while at the same time he couldn't help but find that same refusal…

Intriguing.

With any other woman, he might suspect it to be a ruse —a flirtatious game designed to extract a gesture of undying love. But her response could not be mistaken for anything other than an honest one.

"Very well, then." He swiped his hat off her desk. He'd had quite enough of this woman.

She clasped her hands together beneath her chin and bit her lip. "I refuse to believe you are disappointed."

He could only give her a withering look at such a comment.

"Well then," she echoed his previous sentiment. "I wish you a safe and pleasant journey."

"Pleasant?" He'd not intended his tone to be mocking, but the bruise to his pride was a rather stinging one.

She held his gaze, and he could almost believe he saw a hint of regret in her eyes. "Unforgettable."

He jerked a nod and turned away.

"Goodbye."

Addison very nearly missed the word due to a bell ringing to indicate the change in classes.

With one glance back, he memorized the bright blue color of her eyes, her face, which was more oval than heart-shaped, and the tantalizing bow of her lips. Likely, this would be the last time they spoke to one another.

He would never know the length of the blond hair framing her face or if it felt as soft as he'd imagined.

And that was a very good thing. In fact, it was excellent.

He'd made a lucky escape indeed.

ONE MONTH LATER

"I thought you were returning to Brier Manor after delivering Fiona to school." Rowan's black eyes glanced up from the architectural drawings he'd been examining. Addison had guessed correctly that he would find his brother here, working diligently for all the world as though his living depended on it.

The cot in the corner of the makeshift office proved his brother's ceaseless dedication to this project.

Last winter, Rowan had purchased a broken-down townhouse from a poverty-stricken viscount. He'd wasted no time razing the entire structure in order to build something he swore would put every other Mayfair house to shame.

Addison did not doubt for an instant that Rowan would do precisely that.

"I did. Spent a fortnight with Mother before leaving her to her own devices." Although he loved his mother, as all good sons did, being at home alone with her had proven to be stifling. "She wasn't pleased at my departure."

Addison reached down to rub a hand along Zeus's back while Hera explored the floor around his brother's boots. He'd only weathered his mother's displeasure in order to collect his two most faithful companions to bring along with him to London.

Rowan crouched down and, rubbing her chin, addressed the dog rather than Addison. "Does the duchess have another candidate for your master, sweetheart? Are you excited to have a mother?" Construction dust stood out starkly on Rowan's dark skin, making his brother's eyes appear even blacker than normal.

More than a dozen years had passed since Addison's brother lived as a part of their family, and yet Rowan Stewart, the bastard son of the former Duke of Bedwell, kept well abreast of their affairs.

"Six of them," Addison answered. But for the lack of a marriage certificate between his mother and their father, Rowan would be the one evading such manipulations.

But, unfortunately the pressure for Addison to marry fell squarely on his own shoulders—from both external as well as internal sources. He fully intended to fill a nursery with all sorts of little Briertons—both male and female. But he would do so at his own inclination. Perhaps he'd meet an appropriate lady in the coming spring.

His mother, however, had other ideas. In fact, she had very particular ideas about whom he ought to take as his bride. The very moment she'd handed him a list of names, of ladies listed in order of suitability, he'd made up an excuse to leave for London. He'd allow her to explain his absence when they arrived at Brier Manor, along with their parents, the following week.

Brier Manor was located near the small village of

Bedwellshire, just off the southeast coast of England, making it a few days' drive from London. If he was present when they arrived, he wouldn't have been able to extricate himself without appearing ill-mannered.

Not being there to begin with had eliminated the necessity of such unpleasantness altogether.

Pleasant.

He grimaced at the root of the word, wondering when he could hear it or think it without being reminded of her refusal.

"Their loss is London's gain." Rowan rose and, after a quick glance at his papers, swept his gaze around the makeshift office and then back to Addison. "Care for a tour?"

"I'd feel slighted if you didn't offer." And then asked, "any more problems with vandals?" Trouble had begun shortly after residents of Mayfair became aware of the sale.

His brother ran a hand over his smooth-shaven, brown head. "It ceased for a while but seems to have ramped up again."

"Have you considered posting a guard at night?"

"If it gets any worse, I'll have no choice but to do just that."

One would have thought that in such an exclusive neighborhood, vandals wouldn't be a problem. Unfortunately, Addison realized the vandalism was a result of the very exclusive nature of the neighborhood itself. If the trouble persisted, Addison would hire his own investigator to look into it.

Rowan brushed his hands, as though to dismiss the subject, and then proceeded to lead Addison around a structure that, if the bones were an accurate representation of the end result, was going to be about twice the size of his own townhouse—one that had been built for his grandfather, the Third Duke of Bedwell, nearly a century before.

"Good God, Row, you're building a bloody castle." Addison drifted through an unfinished door onto a terrace balcony. Across the street, trees in Hyde Park dotted the horizon.

Hopefully keeping out of trouble.

"It's an investment." Rowan joined him at the railing, draping his clasped hands over the edge. "Why are you really here, Ad? Leaving the duchess in the lurch like that isn't like you at all."

"I told you." Addison stretched his shoulders uncomfortably.

Rowan didn't answer. When this mansion was completed, Addison surmised that this balcony would be a decent place for one to escape, to retreat from one's duties if only for a few minutes.

But for now, the sounds of workers hammering and shouting instructions at one another made an odd sort of cacophony in the background.

The terrace might also lend itself to more relaxation if one's older brother wasn't staring at him with an all-too-knowing expression.

"Not that I am not always happy at the prospect of your unexpected company, but you've never been inclined to give into impulse. Furthermore, you told me you thought you ought to marry within the next few years and as much as I hate to admit it, your mother seems to only want to assist you in this endeavor."

"She wants to do more than that." Addison thrust aside an unwelcome image of his mother standing at his bedside instructing him on the dos and don'ts of consummation. It was a stretch but not much of one.

"Have you changed your mind altogether, then? You wish to put off marrying?"

"No." Addison clenched and unclenched his fists. He wouldn't put it off, but he would make the decision as to *when*. And more importantly, he, and *only he*, would decide *who*.

"Of course, you haven't. You'll be a good duke and provide no less than three strapping heirs—legitimate heirs —that is." Rowan chuckled.

Addison watched Hera walk around in a few tight circles and then curl up to enjoy the sun. Zeus had already found a spot to lounge.

Relaxing, indeed.

"A young woman refused me a few weeks ago." He surprised himself with the admission.

"Ah. Well then. I was unaware that you were courting anyone. Do I know her?"" His brother ran a hand over his head, which all but gleamed in the sunlight.

"I wasn't courting her. I compromised her."

Rowan raised his brows in disbelief. "Why, you devil. When did this happen?" He obviously found this morsal of information more amusing than Addison had.

"She's one of the teachers at Fiona's school. We were locked in a stairwell together for over an hour. Alone." Saying it out loud made the incident sound even more tawdry than it did in his own mind.

"It's about time you broke a few rules." Rowan sounded quite impressed. "Who is she, some daughter of an earl playing at being a bluestocking?"

"One of Chaswick's half-sisters."

"You offered a teacher, an illegitimate woman, no less, the chance to be your duchess and she said no?"

"That rather sums it up nicely." Addison shoved his hands in his pockets in frustration and paced to the opposite side of the terrace.

"She sounds... interesting." Rowan turned his back on the view, propped his elbows on the railing and narrowed his eyes at Addison. "Do you fancy her, then?"

Did he? "We were alone for over an hour. Asking for her hand was the honorable thing to do." Although if he wasn't smitten, then why did he find himself dwelling on a single kiss weeks later? It was annoying. That's what it was.

"Ah... So there was a scandal then. Why have I not heard about this?"

"There was no scandal." Addison rubbed the back of his neck. "Our situation went undetected. No one knows but the two of us." Which, as he'd told her, made no difference. Only an unscrupulous cad would have failed to offer for her.

"And you, being you, had no choice but to do the honorable thing. Wait... you were *locked* inside of a stairwell? Did you suffer one of your attacks?"

Of all those who knew him, Rowan was the only person who realized the full extent of Addison's weakness.

Addison set his jaw. "I very nearly did. She... She managed to... divert my attention." The memory of the subtle scent of vanilla and mint, along with delicate fingertips drawing lines on his hand was one that had plagued him far too often over the past month.

Rowan watched him, nodding slowly.

"I am considering meeting with Chaswick."

"What do you hope to accomplish by doing this?" This

was why Addison had come to Rowan. Because he would challenge him on any foolish ideas he might have.

"I was not only locked in that stairwell with her, I *kissed* her." And he might have done more if given half the chance.

"You kissed one of Fi's teachers? Is she a beauty then?" Of course, this was what Rowan would home in on.

Was Miss Jones a beauty? Addison hadn't considered her anything more than pretty at first sight, but her looks had improved greatly over the course of their acquaintance.

"Yes."

"What is this delightfully intriguing woman's name?" Addison didn't correct his brother because, for some damnable reason, that was precisely what she'd become to him.

A delightfully intriguing miss...

"Miss Jones." Not for the first time, Addison wondered what her given name might be.

Rowan released a long slow whistle. "Not Delilah, or Medea, or Jezebel, but Miss *Jones*. By God, you must be besotted. I like her already. But as for meeting with the baron, I advise against it."

"Why shouldn't I meet with him?" Rowan's advice was not what Addison wished to hear. Neither did he wish to hear that he was besotted or that Miss Jones was some sort of seductress.

"Meeting with her brother would be irrelevant."

"But I compromised her."

"And she refused your offer. You've fulfilled your duty. What would speaking with her brother accomplish? Force her hand? Do you think you'd enjoy marriage to a woman who wasn't given a choice in the matter?"

His older brother was right, damn him. "I don't mean to

force her hand." And he didn't. But he couldn't shed the feeling that he'd shirked his responsibility somehow.

"What reason did she provide for her refusal?"

Addison had examined her objections from all angles. "She wants to teach, she says. She doesn't want to let the people around her down." But she'd also mentioned that she didn't fit in at the school. As a duchess, she would fit in wherever she wanted to.

Eventually.

"Surely, you of all people must understand this." Rowan pressed.

And somehow, he did.

"Was it bad?" Rowan asked quietly. "The attack? Perhaps that's what this is all about."

Ever since their father had discovered Addison's fears and ridiculed him for them, taking harsh measures to squash them, Rowan had been sympathetic.

Perhaps Rowan had the right of it. Miss Jones had helped him through the experience and something in him wished to hold onto that.

He nodded. "Likely, you're right." Of course, Rowan had the right of it.

Addison ran a hand through his hair. It was the only thing that made sense. He exhaled a shaky breath and, glancing back inside, eagerly dismissed the subject. "When will you be able to move in?"

Rowan seemed as happy to get past it as he was.

"I've yet to decide that I have any desire to reside in Mayfair." Rowan, of course, thrived on being contrary despite most treating him as a prominent member of the *Ton*. Their father would have made life miserable for anyone who hadn't provided his oldest son due respect, and six years after their father's death, Addison would do the same.

But Rowan persisted in rebelling against the trappings that came with mingling amongst society.

Addison gestured around them. "Why bother then? Why not build an equally spectacular monstrosity in a location where you actually do want to live?"

"Because I was offended by the existence of the previous dwelling taking up space on such a magnificent lot." He winked and then disappeared inside.

Addison didn't follow right away but crossed to the ledge and made a second assessment of the distant view as well as the lot itself.

Trees, lawns, and come evening, no doubt the sunset would prove rather spectacular.

Rowan had a point. He had a way of doing that—seeing things others did not. Addison pushed off from the railing and, after a few wrong turns, caught up with his brother who was inspecting one of the workman's efforts. Addison was half-tempted to remove his jacket and go to work beside them but doubted his assistance would be welcomed. Instead, he convinced Rowan to join him at White's the next day, rounded up his dogs, and took his leave.

Only later would he wonder at his decision to make his way back to Bedwell House on foot. Had it been a serendipitous one or merely ironic?

Because, having decided Rowan was correct in advising him to cease his pursuit of Miss Jones, the last person Addison expected to see was strolling along the opposite side of the street, tapping his cane and looking exceedingly satisfied with himself.

"I say, is that you, Bedwell?" Baron Chaswick tipped his

hat and crossed to greet him, and Addison couldn't help but recognize that the man had the same-colored eyes that his sister did. "A happy occasion indeed, stumbling upon you in London. Here for long?"

"A few weeks." The man's question seemed friendly rather than nosey. And as Addison conversed with the baron, he couldn't help but doubt his earlier resolve.

"Excellent. Then you must join my wife and me for dinner before you return to the country. Social pickings are slim this time of year."

Addison had forgotten how charismatic Chaswick was. Apparently, that, in addition to impertinence, must be a family trait.

As they'd been walking in the same direction, the baron matched his steps to Addison's and the two carried on in quiet agreement.

"Met one of your sisters a few weeks ago," Addison offered.

"And how is my sister, the marchioness?" Chaswick slid a questioning glance in Addison's direction.

"Marchioness?" Why would Chaswick think he was discussing Greystone?

"Of Greystone." Chaswick clarified. "I thought they'd have returned to Greystone Manor by now."

For a fraction of a second, Addison's heart dropped. But then he realized Chaswick was referring to the other sister —the one who'd taken full advantage of her opportunity to enter society.

"Oh, no. You misunderstand. I met Miss Jones while establishing my sister at Miss Primm's. Your sister *is* a teacher there, is she not?"

"Was." Chaswick pounded his cane with more force than

necessary onto the walk. "Until a fortnight ago. Apparently, a thousand-pound donation is insufficient to replace half a school of students."

Addison halted and turned, startling Chaswick into stopping as well. "She's no longer employed? What happened?"

"Mrs. Eunice Metcalf happened," the baron all but growled. "The meddling blabbermouth decided my sister wasn't proper enough to teach her frail-minded daughters. Suggested she was a bad influence and stirred up a handful of other parents into believing the same."

"A bad influence?" Had someone, in fact, witnessed her hasty escape from the stairwell? Had word gotten out that he had not been trapped alone?

Damned busybody gossips. But... if that was the case, wouldn't Chaswick have challenged him already?

Addison certainly would have if the tables had been turned. *Unless he did not know the identity of the gentleman she'd been trapped with.*

He scratched his chin. Would that not have been common knowledge? Perhaps he didn't understand the machinations of women's minds as well as he thought he did.

"It's not as though Collette had any control over it," Chaswick replied. Control over the situation in the stairwell?

"Dashed shame." Addison murmured. A fortnight. That would mean she'd been sacked little over a week after he, himself had taken his leave.

"Of course, she's innocent in all of it. But that Metcalf woman didn't stop there. No, she insisted her primary concern was Collette's lack of teaching experience—implied that she wasn't capable of controlling her classroom. After only one week. By God, Bedwell, my sisters have not had an easy time of things, as I'm sure you'll understand. But it wasn't as though Collette had any designs on raising her social status. Trust me, if that Mrs. Metcalf deigns to show her face in London next spring, she'll find her salver tray surprisingly empty."

Chaswick exhaled a disgusted huff as he literally marched along the street beside him, Zeus and Hera dancing along in excitement.

Collette. French, meaning *People of victory.* The name was a strong one but also feminine. It suited her.

"Nothing could have hurt my sister more." Chaswick's words pricked Addison's conscience—even if he had not been the reason for her dismissal. But why else would she have been considered a bad influence?

"What will she do now?" But of course, she'd been innocent. If she hadn't been, she would have locked onto his proposal like a dog with a bone.

Even if she had been guilty of setting the trap, that wouldn't have altered the fact that he'd taken advantage of her.

Addison ought to have remained in the area for a few days to assure himself of her well-being before he left. At the very least, he ought to have provided his directions so she could contact him if necessary. Or if she'd changed her mind.

But her refusal had been adamant.

"She's back with us at Byrd House for now. Bethany— my baroness—has had some success consoling her. If anyone understands the weight of scandal, let me assure you, my wife does. Collette insists she still wants to teach and I've an offer of another post for her to consider, but I'm none too confident that it's the sort of position she wants. Metcalf's wagging tongue has all but assured no one within a hundred-mile radius wants to take her on. *Blasted woman.*"

And now, Miss Collette Jones had one less choice. Addison's initial inclination was to accompany Chaswick back to Byrd House—offer for her again. It was, in fact, the honorable thing to do. And he was an honorable gentleman, above all else.

But she had laughed outright at his first proposal, and then run away and hidden when Miss Shipley discovered the stairwell was locked.

She'd described his kiss as *pleasant.*

She had not even entertained his offer nor had the courage to look him in the eye when she'd given him her answer.

"I have no wish to marry you... I give you leave to return to your ducal life knowing that you have done that which is honorable by me. But please... Please, I beg of you to keep this to yourself."

She had adamantly insisted she knew what was best.

He and Chaswick arrived at a crossroads and the baron turned to walk in the opposite direction of Bedwell Place. "I apologize for exhorting you with my troubles." He shrugged. "Every last male of my acquaintance, it seems, has retired to the country for the winter, and I am desperate for masculine company. Care to practice foils some afternoon? Billiards? Or, by god, even a good game of cards."

Miss Jones, Collette, *is here in London.*

"Indeed," Addison answered. "It's been too long since I've sparred."

"Say, what are you doing this evening? Unless you've

other plans, my wife is hosting a dinner party. You're more than welcome to join us. And later this week we'll meet up at White's."

The dinner party wasn't the visit Addison had in mind. But Rowan had been right in that it wouldn't be fair of him to force her hand. He would speak with her tonight. Likely she'd all but beg him to renew his offer.

After that, he'd meet with Chaswick officially, tomorrow morning.

Collette.

"What time shall I come?"

"Eight o'clock."

As her brother disappeared down the walk, Addison again wondered at the coincidence of running into him. And for the split second before he could dismiss such ridiculousness, entertained the notion that it could be fate.

"Woof!" Zeus checked Addison's train of thought with a well-timed admonishment.

"Don't look at me that way." He scowled at his dog. "I was only joking."

∾

"If Chase doesn't hear back from any of the schools he's contacted by the end of the week, I believe I will join Sarah at Easter Park," Collette admitted quietly. She knew it was not what Bethany wanted to hear but she'd been contemplating her future ever since her last meeting with Miss Primm.

"My preference, Miss Jones, would be to keep you on." The headmistress removed her spectacles and rubbed the bridge of her nose. "And I'll admit I wish I could say 'good riddance' to the

Metcalfs and everyone else raising such a stink. But I must consider all of my students, and my other teachers. It would be irresponsible of me to put the entire school at risk."

"You're letting me go?" Collette's heart fell to her shoes. She could hardly believe it. This was her dream. Her students were just now beginning to engage with some enthusiasm.

"I'm sorry. I've arranged for your wages to go to you for the entire term, because none of this is fair... And I'll have to speak with Chaswick, of course." The woman donned her spectacles and stared at her with sympathetic eyes. "You have the makings of an excellent teacher. I do hope you won't let this derail your aspirations."

And later, when Miss Shipley had walked her out the front door. "This isn't the end for you, Miss Jones. Would you believe me if I admitted to being jealous of you? You have a loyal family, and they esteem you greatly. Someday you'll look back on this nasty business with your reputation and realize it only made you stronger."

"Collette? Her sister-in-law's voice jerked her out of the unpleasant memory—one she'd replayed in her mind several times since.

"Just... wool gathering." Collette blinked away the stinging in her eyes. Because, *of course, it had derailed her aspirations.* How could it not have? And as of yet, she did not feel any stronger than she had before.

Quite the opposite, rather.

"You must know that we love having you here!" Bethany set her embroidery aside and frowned. After Diana's excellent match last spring, Collette had labored under no misconception that her sister-in-law still held out hope for her. In fact, Collette was certain that's what all of this new clothing and the visit from a stylist had been about.

Bethany smiled conspiratorially. "And... I wasn't going to mention anything yet, since it's still early, but..." She settled her hand over her abdomen in an unmistakably protective manner.

"A baby?" Collette raised her brows. "You're expecting a baby?"

Bethany nodded. "Yes!"

"But that's wonderful!" Collette jumped out of her chair and all but leapt across the room so she was sitting beside the woman who'd embraced Chase's second family so completely. "When? Does Chase know?"

Bethany shook her head and laughed. "My courses are only two weeks late, and I wanted to be sure. But I've felt queasy in the mornings and I just... I just know that I am. I was going to tell him this evening, but we have guests coming for dinner. I was thinking of going away for a few days, to Brighton, just the two of us, and I'd hoped you'd keep her ladyship occupied."

Although not mad, exactly, Chase's mother occasionally suffered states of mental confusion. And although she could recall memories from decades before, sometimes didn't remember that her own husband had been dead for over six years now.

Chase provided the very best of nurses, but he and Bethany were reluctant to leave the dowager baroness alone for more than a day.

"Of course, I will," Collette answered, wishing already that she wouldn't have to wait until the following summer to become an aunt. "He is going to be so happy and make for the best father in the world. Besides that, you two could have some time alone."

"But I don't want to take advantage of you."

"You never have! Even if you did, you'd have every right —what with all that you and Chase have done for Diana and Sarah and me—even for mother. I'm just so excited for both of you."

Collette spent the next hour asking all sorts of questions about the changes she was going to experience, how Bethany would feel if the child was a girl or if it was a boy, and then both commiserated with one another for missing their sisters and their own mothers. So much had changed for all of them over the past year.

"Where will you spend the end of your confinement? Here? I'd think your mother will wish to be with you."

"I'm not so sure about that." Bethany tapped each of her fingers onto her thumb, doing her counting thing that she did whenever she wasn't completely comfortable. She was the eldest daughter of the Earl of Westerley, and her mother, the dowager countess, wasn't the warmest of ladies. "But for now I need to finalize my plans for Chase. I imagine the weather will have cooled too much for us to bathe in the sea, but I'm looking forward to the fresh air."

Embroidery all but forgotten, both ladies faced one another, feet propped on the settee between them and discussed every detail that popped into their minds.

When a contented silence fell, Collette smiled. She'd been devastated to be sent away from Miss Primm's and today was the first time in nearly a month that she'd felt happy about anything.

Bethany leaned forward and squeezed her hand. "I am so glad to see you smile again. Your *genuine* smile, not the strained one you've had since you came back from Miss Primm's. I'll have to remember when you are feeling low, all I need to do is promise you a niece or nephew and you perk right up." There were times her sister-in-law could practically read her mind.

"Is that Collette laughing, by chance?" Chase stepped inside, looking as handsome as ever, if not a little windblown. From the moment Collette had first met her brother, shortly after their father's death, she'd been drawn to his charisma and warmth. Nothing had legally compelled him to even so much as acknowledge their relationship. In fact, he'd had every reason to ignore their very existence. But instead, he'd not only accepted them, but he'd eventually invited them into his life. Chase had brought sunshine in a time of mourning, and she would forever be grateful to him for that.

She owed him everything.

"I'm hopeful we hear that sound more often." Bethany didn't miss a beat as she tilted her head back for her husband's kiss.

"It has been rather quiet around here now that Diana's married," Chase commented, absentmindedly clasping his wife's hand in a way that allowed his fingertips to tap along hers. "You'll be happy to hear, Collette, the father of an old friend from Eton has extended an offer for you to teach at the village school near his estate. It seems the woman who'd formerly held the position has run off with the local blacksmith and they're willing to take almost anyone."

"Not just anyone, of course." Bethany corrected him, wincing. "Any school would be lucky to have Collette. Since she's been here, I have an entirely new appreciation for Latin."

"As have I. Unfortunately, I doubt they'll place much importance on that." He held up a finger. "But it is a legitimate post, and they don't care one wit about Collette's position in society."

Collette frowned. She'd felt like an utter nobody ever since returning to London, and that hadn't bothered her, but... "Exactly where is this school, and when must I provide them with my answer?"

Now it was Chase's turn to wince. "Dumbarton. He says they need an answer as soon as possible.

"Dumbarton? *As in the far reaches of Scotland?*" Bethany's dismay echoed Collette's.

If she accepted a post in Scotland, Collette would be several days' drive from everyone she'd ever cared about and everything that was familiar to her. For the first time, and for very practical reasons *only*, she almost wished she'd accepted the Duke of Bedwell's proposal.

Almost.

It seemed she was running out of options. *Electio, optio.* But she stopped such thoughts before allowing herself to fall into a bout of self-pity.

She was not completely without choices.

"It's too far," Bethany said, but Collette felt her brother's watchful gaze.

"Is it too far, Cole? You don't have to take it. You are always welcome here—you know that. We could try bringing you out again next spring." She shot him a glare and he added, "Or not."

She could not, however, depend on her brother forever.

But... *Scotland?* And not a town that was anywhere near the border—but very, very distant Scotland.

She'd miss everything—and everyone! She'd miss spending the holidays with Sarah and her mother. She'd miss the birth of her first niece or nephew! She might as well move to the Americas!

"He and his wife plan to leave London a week from tomorrow. They're happy to take you back with them at that time." Chase rubbed his chin thoughtfully. "To be perfectly honest, Cole, I'll be disappointed if you take it. Not disappointed in you, but for myself, for us, as we would miss and worry about you every day. Perhaps you'll see things differently after spending a pleasant evening entertaining our guests. No one will judge you if you change your mind about teaching. A night spent in the company of others might be just the diversion you need to gain a new perspective."

Not likely. The prospect of several hours making polite conversation and avoiding Bethany's matchmaking was not one Collette looked forward to.

"About that. I was thinking I'd make myself scarce in my chamber—"

"Are you ill?" Chase asked, brows raised. "Because if you are not, we would appreciate your participation to keep the numbers even." Her brother moved farther into the room and then dropped onto a high-back chair, draping one leg over the other in the lazy manner that only aristocrats and scholars got away with.

"Since when have you cared about even numbers?" But Collette was already resigned. Because, truly, there was nothing she wouldn't do for her brother.

"Since my wife cares about such things."

"I'm sorry, Collette." Bethany had also become one of those people for whom Collette would do anything. And come next summer, there'd be yet another one—one who weighed less than a stone and would have the softest of skin and downy fine hair. She couldn't help but grin when Bethany met her eyes.

"As it's only one evening and since the two of you are in such *dire* need—" Collette dramatically raised the back of her hand to her forehead "—I will join you and your guests for dinner." She dropped her hand and grinned. "It's not as though I have nothing to wear."

No doubt, one of their guests would be an impoverished, not-quite-repulsive baron or baronet who just happened to be in search of a wife. Collette didn't even want to know the price her brother had put on her head.

Or dowry, rather.

Not that Chase would ever be called upon to pay it.

But if Bethany wished Collette to attend her dinner party, Collette would make her very best effort to be pleasant. It was the least she could do for the woman who was going to make her an aunt sometime late next spring.

Besides, it was only a dinner party.

~

As Collette bathed and then dressed for the evening, she changed her mind, and then changed her mind back at least a dozen times regarding the teaching position in Scotland.

Staring into the mirror as Bethany's lady's maid inserted a jeweled pin into her hair, she wondered at the ironies in life. Her brother could provide her with everything most ladies wanted—security, fineries, family—and yet one mean-spirited woman had been capable of crushing her dream. It wasn't fair that simple spite from someone like Mrs. Metcalf could upend Collette's life so completely.

"You look stunning in blue—especially this shade." Polly

smoothed the sleeve of Collette's gown and then added one last pin to secure her coiffure. "All my life I wished I had hair like yours—so light, like the sunshine."

"My youngest sister once told me it reminded her of the morning sun on her face." Collette had almost forgotten about that. Sarah had said Collette's hair was softer, finer, and Diana's, which was thicker and heavier, reminded her of night.

"From what her ladyship has told me, Miss Sarah is doing well with her new teacher." Polly stepped back approvingly. "And such a relief to have Miss Diana married off. The rest of the staff and I were beyond pleased at such a happy occasion—to be certain."

Collette agreed that Diana's wedding had been a happy occasion but... *a relief?* The maid's comment seemed odd. "The servants were concerned?"

Polly pulled out a pin and swirled a strand of Collette's blondish hair in a different direction. "Even as a baron, his lordship was taking a risk by claiming... I mean, by bringing the two of you out..." The maid fell silent, seemingly reconsidering her words.

But Collette spun around, confused. "What do you mean?" She'd been under the impression that the only reason he'd not claimed them publicly before had been because of his mother's sensibilities.

"My apologies, Miss, I'm speaking out of turn." Polly finished Collette's coiffure and went about fussing with some jewelry on the other side of the room. "Now where did those slippers go?"

Bethany's guests were due to arrive shortly and although Collette would have liked to question the maid further, she hurriedly slipped on the shoes purchased to match her gown, took one last glance in the looking glass, and brushed at her skirts.

Unsettled by the idea that Chase had risked more than his mother's peace, which had been considerable indeed, Collette entered the withdrawing room at the precise moment the knocker sounded from the front foyer. She would ask Bethany about it later.

"By God, Collette, you look stunning. What have you done with yourself?" Chase crossed to a side table. "Sherry?"

"Yes, please." What had he risked for them? He'd never said a word. Had he had to pay to bring them into society, much as he'd paid in order for Miss Primm to hire her?

"Isn't Cerulean a bold color for a debutante?" Chase handed her the glass with a wink. "It's a shame we couldn't invent a dead husband for you. I rather think you could make quite a splash as a widow, holding salons, poetry readings, and whatnot. Everyone in London would be smarter for knowing you. Don't you agree, my love?" He addressed the last to his wife.

"I know of a few octogenarian bachelors." Bethany leveled a thoughtful gaze in her direction, giving Collette pause to wonder if her sister-in-law was only half-joking.

"With my luck, he'd end up a centurion," Collette muttered just as Chase's attention focused on the doorway behind her.

"Hawthorne, good to see you. And you, My Lady. Welcome!" Her brother's voice spurred Collette to turn around to share in welcoming the first guests to arrive. She'd met the high-ranking couple on a few occasions last spring and found the countess to be friendly and engaging, and her earl to be quiet, but with a kind look in his eyes. By the time Chase was pouring them drinks, a second couple arrived. The Marquess and Marchioness of Rockingham. Bethany had explained that the Marchioness, a very proper and distinguished lady, was involved in the funding of London's largest foundling hospital. The woman was a few years older than Collette and Bethany and had an almost intimidating quality about her.

As more guests arrived, Collette edged toward the back of the room while Bethany made introductions, smiling and being the perfect hostess.

These people were so very different from Collette. They were pleasant enough, but she could never dismiss the awareness that these people were genuine members of society, whereas, she... was not. Collette dropped her gaze to study her hands when a shiver drifted down her spine.

"Bedwell. Good to see you could make it."

"My pleasure, Chaswick."

There was no mistaking that voice, even from across the room. Collette lifted her lashes and felt a zing of awareness when she found herself staring into his icy-blue gaze.

But if it was icy, why did it send bolts of flames coursing through her?

AN UNLIKELY COINCIDENCE

Of all the people in London, what was the Duke of Bedwell doing here? And why was her brother leading him across the room to where she was standing?

"Collette, I believe you've met His Grace? Bedwell, you know my sister, Miss Jones." It was a wonder Collette remembered to drop into a curtsey as Chase presented her. The memory of the duke's lips brushing hers flashed through her mind. And another of him bending over her bare hand, when she'd been a respectable teacher at a respectable school—and then later, in a stairwell, when he'd taken her into his arms and—

"Under considerably different circumstances." The formal tone of his voice shouldn't send vibrations shooting through her like they did. What on earth was the matter with her?

"Indeed," Collette agreed. Why had he come? He'd agreed to keep what happened in the stairwell between the two of them. Was it possible that his sudden appearance in her brother's drawing room was merely a coincidence?

"I hadn't realized you'd left Miss Primm's until recently." His statement was a grim-sounding one. She'd forgotten the effect his unsmiling demeanor had on her. It ought to be off-putting but it wasn't. Her brother didn't seem bothered by it either.

Chase's attention drifted to movement at the door. "Ah, more guests have arrived. Bedwell, I'll surrender you into my sister's capable hands, if you'll excuse me."

All politeness, Chase sauntered away, leaving only the hint of his familiar cologne in his wake as he did so. Leaving Collette alone with the duke—a man who'd entered her thoughts on more occasions than she wished to admit, even to herself, over the past month.

Collette shifted her gaze around the room before bringing it back to rest on the duke. His hair was longer than it had been the last time they'd been in one another's company but other than that he was just as dukish as when she'd first met him. Perhaps even more so.

"I was sacked." She raised her shoulders and then dropped them. "It wasn't my choice to leave."

"That is most unfortunate." But he sounded rather unsympathetic.

Was he deliberately being cruel or was he simply obtuse? Since he didn't seem like a thick-skulled individual, she determined it was the former.

"Yes, in fact, it *was* most unfortunate," she rejoined.

His eyes widened. "Do you think I'm being glib?"

Collette pinched her lips together and nodded.

"I am not, as a matter of fact. While going through my mail this very afternoon, I discovered a letter posted by my sister—a letter in which she wrote of her displeasure over the termination of her favorite teacher. She wrote that she had been quite enjoying your class and was very, very disappointed when you left. Which she emphasized to me using Latin words, mind you. *Ut destitute*," he said. "Apparently, while you were there, you made something of an impression—on at least one of your students."

Collette narrowed her eyes at him. Was he teasing her?

"You do not believe me?" he queried.

Collette had only been able to teach for one week before Mrs. Metcalf's objections took on a life of their own. She had hoped she'd imparted something to her students in that short time.

Ut destitute. Very disappointed.

Lady Fiona had been one who had paid close attention. She'd also asked questions and mentioned that although she'd known it was important to learn Latin, no one had ever explained it to her in a way that made her believe it. No one had ever told her why Latin was such an important language.

"I was most disappointed to leave," she admitted. An understatement, to be certain.

She wished she could be angry at Miss Primm, or consider herself a martyr, but the fact was, the circumstances surrounding her very personhood would follow her throughout her life. It had been naïve to think that the parents of social-climbing students would accept her—no matter how much money Chase donated to the school.

"I was unaware of your changed circumstances until today. It was simply by chance that I happened upon your brother." He hadn't sounded unsympathetic before but perhaps that was simply... him.

"It was all rather sudden." Collette grimaced, blinking back the unwanted stinging in her eyes. She forced her mouth into what she hoped resembled a pleasant smile. "Otherwise, your sister is doing well? She is happy at Miss Primm's *plebeian institution?*"

The duke met her gaze with a level stare and then cocked one brow. "Presently, yes."

Collette nodded and then rolled her lips together. That gaze of his, which ought to leave her cold but didn't, flicked to her mouth and then up to her eyes again.

The effect of his perusal was disconcerting, but it was also... exhilarating.

"I would have come sooner if I'd known. I have every intention of meeting with your brother..."

Collette stared up at him, confused. They'd already been over this. She'd released him from any responsibility he felt toward her.

She searched his impassive expression for any sign as to what he was thinking. A tick in his jaw gave away... something. He was not as unaffected as he seemed. But why?

"How are you?" He asked.

How was she?

His question seemed to reach inside of her chest and squeeze her heart, and she didn't know why.

For an instant, she found herself staring at his mouth. His lips appeared firm and set just now, as they'd been at the onset of the kiss they'd shared. But he'd softened them gradually, like early snow beneath a warm autumn sun.

"Miss Jones?"

"I am... fine." She was not really. But when a person asked how you were, Bethany had explained to her that one never actually answered truthfully.

∾

ADDISON'S THROAT THICKENED. How had he not realized how lovely she was? Or had she intentionally downplayed her looks while at the school?

Tonight she wore a gown of brilliant blue silk, although not as blue as her eyes. And rather than the tight chignon she'd worn before, delicate curls framed her face and a few silky strands looped flirtatiously around her neck.

Jolted by an unexpected surge of attraction, he skimmed his gaze around the others in the room and inhaled a slow calming breath.

He was acquainted in some way or another with all of Chaswick's guests, and he likely would only be allowed a few more minutes, if that, to speak to her alone.

Contrary to the answer she gave him, it was obvious that she was *not* fine. Having lived with women, whether they be his mother, his sister, or even one of the servants, he'd learned that the word *fine* most definitely did not mean *fine*.

Best to get this over with quickly. He stepped forward and bent his head closer, for a hint of privacy.

"It is my fault that you lost your employment. I intend to meet with your brother tomorrow." Tiny earbobs shaped like hearts dangled alongside a few golden tendrils. He licked his lips and then, remembering Rowan's advice, flicked his stare to meet her eyes. "If you have no objections."

"Meet with Chase? But that isn't necessary. We discussed this already…"

"Perhaps that was true last month." Addison skimmed one hand along her arm. "But in light of your dismissal from Miss Primm's, surely, you feel differently." He'd not expected her persistent contrariness—although he should have. "Allow me to do the honorable thing here."

"But my circumstances have nothing to do with you."

"They have everything to do with me. Miss Primm dismissed you because of complaints that you were not suitably upstanding."

"Yes, but—"

"I don't know who let it out, and when I do, I'll take them to task myself. But in lieu of your dismissal, I assumed that you, an educated woman, would see fit to reconsider your answer."

She tilted her head, and her scent tickled his senses. But the incredulous light in her eyes reminded him of the look she'd given him when they'd been locked in the stairwell. As though she wasn't quite certain he wasn't dicked in the knob.

"Nothing is out that wasn't already public." She cast an anxious glance behind her. "No one knows about... what happened between you and me."

"Then why...?" He ran a hand through his hair. "Why were you expelled? Did you get yourself caught in some other scandal following my departure?" Good God, if that was the case, Miss Primm had had a perfect right to let her go. "Is there someone else?"

"Oh, heavens, no." She frowned. "The scandal I was expelled for occurred over twenty years ago."

Twenty years ago? "Because of your father?"

"Mrs. Metcalf, one of the mothers, has wanted me gone since the moment she realized who I was."

Chaswick had mentioned Mrs. Metcalf's part in all this. Collette's brother had been more than angry; he'd been livid.

Addison remembered the woman. In fact, she was one of

89

the reasons he hadn't wanted to abandon Fiona there. Clutching, climbing, manipulative…

Miss Jones grimaced, drawing his attention to her mouth. *Collette.* Now *that* was the name of a seductress… Although her brand of charm wasn't something a woman could conjure.

"She feared my illegitimacy would rub off on one of her daughters. Three days following your departure, she brought a petition to Miss Primm—signed by some twenty or so of the other parents."

"But Miss Primm was aware of your circumstances when she hired you." It wasn't as though she'd been teaching at Eton or Oxford. Although not often, he had witnessed members of society treat his brother similarly, and his gut tightened at the thought of Collette having to endure such censure alone.

"She was faced with losing a third of her students if she were to keep me on. I don't blame her. I definitely don't blame you." She shrugged and Addison's gaze dropped to the delicate curve where her neck sloped into her shoulders. Vanilla. He'd all but tasted it there.

Her scandal had nothing to do with him, but the fact remained that he'd been alone with her in that stairwell, and that he'd kissed her. Regardless of who knew, his own conscience would plague him forever if he didn't right her circumstances somehow.

And the most effective way to do that was to marry her. The notion that he was going to have to convince her of this was absurd.

"Your brother was not happy about it." In the little time he'd spent with Chaswick, it was obvious that the baron doted on his sisters.

"I feel horrible for letting him down." But she had not let her brother down, in truth. She'd done nothing wrong.

"He doesn't blame you."

"But he should. Will you answer something for me?" Without waiting for a response, she went on. "What all did he risk by acknowledging me and my sisters the way he did? With society, I mean?"

Her candor, he realized, was a part of her charm. Addison considered Chaswick's position, his rank, and his wealth. Still... "He cannot have known, really," he answered. "Society is a fickle but often unforgiving institution."

Her eyes widened and then her expression all but collapsed into dismay. "But what *exactly* was he risking? Friendships?"

Any gently bred lady would know precisely what her brother had risked. Acceptance amongst the British elite was something one mustn't ever take for granted. Although not a tangible thing, once lost, it was rarely bestowed again. This hierarchy of power permeated the very air that they breathed.

Her eyes held a hint of pleading, and Addison sensed an inkling of why she'd refused him.

Because she was not, in truth, gently bred. She'd been raised in a cloak of secrecy.

"Your brother's title is an old one, and he's always been well respected." He would explain this to her. "And for that, he possesses considerable influence. But think of that influence as money."

"Diana made a good match." She tilted her head and two lines appeared between her eyes.

"Upon which some of that influence was returned to him."

Miss Jones blinked a few times as she seemed to grasp what he was telling her. "Are my failures bankrupting his influence?"

"Not hardly." Addison stared pointedly across the room to where the baron and baroness conversed easily with the Marquess and Marchioness of Rockingham. "And he wouldn't have done it if he hadn't wanted to."

"But my presence in London now cannot be helping." Her bottom lip quivered. "I knew before that it could not be easy for Chaswick and... but now that I've been dismissed from a such a reputable institution as Miss Primm's..."

"There are things you'll never have any control over."

"This should not be one of them." Her eyes took on a distant look, and he could practically feel the energy of her brain working to come up with her own solution.

"Have you always been so independent?" he asked.

"It's not that I'm independent, it's that I'm realistic. Other people won't always be there to take care of my problems, to take care of my mother, and my sisters. If I don't take care of them, who will?"

Because her father had had another family. "But you have your brother," Addison pointed out.

"Nothing is guaranteed." Her voice had fallen to almost a whisper. She wanted to trust in other people but couldn't. Her independence was her cornerstone.

Getting a glimpse of the steely strength lurking in such a feminine package altered his view of her. She didn't want to be taken care of. Was that what drove her passion for teaching?

"I suppose I ought to take the position in Scotland then."

"Scotland?" *What the devil?*

"I've been offered a position at a village school in Dumbarton. I wasn't going to take it because... Well, it's so very far. But considering what you've just told me—"

"You aren't going to Scotland." It was true that by marrying her, his own standing would temporarily lose a hint of its luster, but as far as she and her brother were concerned, such a union would be considered a notable achievement. Having a sister as a duchess would not only reestablish her brother's standing but lift it higher than it had been before.

"That won't be necessary," he added.

"But if what you say is true, it would be selfish of me to remain here in London with them." Her eyes clouded with concern now, and she clutched his arm. Even through his shirt and jacket, her touch jolted him. It had him wanting to close the distance between them and identify which floral scent accompanied the sweetness of vanilla and mint.

"There's another way for you to help them. If you—"

"Dinner is served." Chaswick's manservant chose a most inconvenient moment to make his announcements.

"Going to Scotland is the best way. I—I hadn't realized. I mean, I suppose I knew, deep down." The other guests in the room were moving about, pairing up with one another to escort or be escorted into the dining room.

He'd flustered her and that hadn't been his intention at all. He'd merely thought...

"If I am not mistaken, Lady Sheffield awaits your escort into the dining room." Collette pointed out, lifting her chin, looking quite brave and really...

Rather magnificent.

"Come driving with me tomorrow." He was going about this all wrong.

"But should I be seen? I don't want to cost Chase and

Bethany any more influence than I already have. I'll remain at home until it's time for me to leave for Scotland."

"You aren't going to Scotland." He covered her hand with his.

"But—"

"I'll collect you at two o'clock." He barely managed to get the words out before Lady Chaswick appeared at their side, along with the indomitable Lady Sheffield and an older gentleman Addison didn't recognize.

Collette jerked her hand out from under his but not in time for such a curious gesture between a duke and an unemployed teacher to escape the two ladies' notice.

"Your Grace?" Lady Chaswick made all the proper introductions. The man was Sir Grimsley, recently of Herefordshire, and based purely upon Lady Chaswick's cunning expression, Addison had little doubt the man had been invited for the sole purpose of meeting Collette.

Frustrated to have been interrupted before matters were settled, but willing to wait to discuss it with her under more appropriate circumstances, Addison offered his elbow to the grand lady staring at him curiously.

And as he escorted Lady Sheffield into the dining room, he was certain on one account. Miss Collette Jones was not going to be traveling to Scotland. Not if he had anything to say about it.

Nor was she going to be courted by this Grimsley fellow.

~

COLLETTE HAD ALWAYS THOUGHT the reason Chase hadn't brought them out in public before had been to protect his mother's sensibilities. How had she not realized that he had put his own position in society at risk?

Sitting through dinner her mind wandered all too easily. At least twice, Sir Grimsley, who Collette realized was the actual victim of Bethany's matchmaking efforts, had had to repeat a question or comment he'd directed at her. He was pleasant enough, despite his advanced age, which she assumed was somewhere between forty and sixty, but...

"I imagine you were pleased to escape that place... that Miss Primm's school for girls." Sir Grimsley wrinkled his nose. "Not that teaching isn't a noble endeavor, my dear, but I cannot help but opine that you would be far happier raising your own family."

"But I was not pleased. I was most disappointed." She spoke without thinking and hastily added, "Although you are correct in that *most* ladies prefer to have families of their own."

"Indeed," he commented, leaning closer. In that moment, she knew that, rather than move to Scotland, if she wished to, she could marry Sir Grimsley—or someone like him.

She was not *completely* without choices.

When Collette had become old enough to understand that her father lived with another family, and that that was not at all normal, she'd asked her mother how she could love a man who'd put them in such a situation. Her mother had told her that it had been her *choice*. She could marry a poor man, she'd told Collette, one who was just as likely to be unfaithful, or she could be mistress to a rich one and live a life of considerable luxury. Her mother had insisted that women did, contrary to common misconception, have *choices*.

The choices weren't always what she hoped for, but they were hers to make.

Lord Grimsley was a choice. Scotland was a choice. Staying on as a companion to her sister-in-law might be a choice. She could even go to Easter Park and live with her mother and Sarah in the country.

The only option that was not at all viable was the duke's outlandish proposal.

Not only did she lack what was required to be a duchess, she couldn't begin to fathom what that was.

She snuck a peek down the table to where he sat at the opposite end, and almost as though he'd been waiting for that moment, he caught her with his cool gaze.

Three full seconds passed, three seconds of tingling awareness, before she could tear her stare away.

He was not like any other man she'd ever met. And not simply because he was a duke.

He had an unrelenting sense of honor and responsibility, and although incomprehensible, she couldn't help but admire him for it. She knew far too well that such a quality in an aristocrat was rare. It likely had more to do with his character *as a person* than his actual position.

How many of his equals saw beyond his title to the man inside? How many of them realized he was just as vulnerable as anyone? Few, if any. And it was likely he wanted it that way.

But whether he'd wanted to or not, he'd shown that part of himself to her. And—Collette stared at her half-eaten plate—doing that had been good for him. No one should go through life hiding the person that they really were.

The realization caused her more than a little regret to have to refuse him.

If only he was a shopkeeper, an artist, or another teacher —or even a baronet. But a duke!

He had told her she was not going to be traveling to Scotland. He had suggested that he wanted to meet with Chase.

Was he mad? She was barely accepted amongst the circles of those who knew her as a baron's sister. Did he truly believe society would accept her as a duchess?

He'd explained that power and influence had value. Were his coffers so full that they wouldn't be affected by marrying so far beneath him? Because as much as she wished it, no one would forget who she was—what she was. Eventually, he would regret his unrelenting compulsion to uphold his honor. His entire family would be affected. Along with their children.

She shook her head. Why on earth was she even contemplating the idea?

"Would you like that, my dear?" Lord Grimsley touched her arm, and for the third time over the course of their conversation, she had to ask him to repeat his question.

"I'm sorry. Wool-gathering." But in making her apology, she realized how insulting the admission was. What man in his right mind would want to make her his wife?

He merely smiled and nodded vaguely, and she realized that it wasn't *her* that he wanted, in truth, but the dowry her brother would provide.

"Would you like to go driving with me tomorrow afternoon?"

Choices.

Bedwell had threatened to collect her at two.

Choices.

"I'm afraid I have a prior commitment," she answered,

"but perhaps another day?" If she hadn't left for Scotland yet.

The very thought of being so far from her family sent her heart dropping. If she took the position, she'd be lucky to visit with her sisters even once a year. Seeing Diana and Sarah and her mother would be a major undertaking. She would miss out on knowing all the new things Sarah learned when already she was itching to ask her about the reading and to meet this special dog—all of that and also to warn her about the bogs. Who would warn her about the bogs?

She would miss Bethany and Chase, and she would miss her new niece or nephew.

She wouldn't be able to visit Diana in her new home with the marquess. Her sister would move on, likely begin having babies of her own and she wouldn't have Collette to discuss her doubts or fears.

Collette would miss all of it.

Panic shot through her. Scotland sounded like more of a prison sentence than a choice.

Perhaps she would discover she had more choices tomorrow after driving with the duke. He'd told her he'd liked the kiss.

Was it possible he had something else in mind altogether? Was he contemplating a less than honorable proposal?

But then why would he speak to her brother about it?

By the time dinner was over and the ladies rose to withdraw in order to allow the men to take their port, Collette's mind had twisted itself up in knots.

One moment, she was contemplating teaching a class full of students in the far reaches of Scotland, the next, she was contemplating becoming a mistress. It had been good enough for her mother, surely it was something she ought to at least consider?

Or maybe she was wrong in imagining that. Lady Fiona had enjoyed learning Latin from her. And the duke wasn't all that enamored with the idea of his sister attending Miss Primm's.

Collette froze. Surely, that was it. He wanted to hire her to tutor his sister! Strolling along the corridor to the drawing room, she found herself feeling foolish. Likely this scenario had the most merit.

A moment after Collette stepped into the drawing room, Bethany met her gaze and then raised one brow, as though asking a question. Bethany had not missed the fact that the Duke of Bedwell's hand had been on hers and her hand had been clutching his arm.

Collette merely shook her head and then shrugged.

Because she, herself, had more questions than answers.

SUITABLE YOUNG LADIES

"*H*era made dinner out of one of your new boots. I'll order a new pair made up tomorrow," Mr. Brown informed Addison with just the proper amount of consternation. Addison's mother had hired Mr. Brown to valet for him six years ago. In fact, Brown had taken up his duties the day after Addison reached his majority—precisely two weeks before his father was killed in a duel. This was not the first pair of boots that had ended its usefulness in such a manner.

Doubtless, it would be the last.

"I'm sure she enjoyed them more than I did." Addison much preferred his older pair, which had been broken in years ago and all but conformed to the shape of his foot. "How many pairs is that now, eh, Hera?" Addison addressed the smaller of his canine pals, who curled up beside Zeus on his bed where both of them watched his every move now that he'd returned home for the night.

"Four pairs now, Your Grace," Brown answered for the

energetic English Foxhound. "I shall save the remaining one for the next time you go out for the evening. Did you enjoy yourself tonight, Your Grace?"

"I did," Addison said, turning to the side as his valet assisted him in removing his jacket. He attended most dinner parties out of duty but this one had been somewhat different, less stilted. And although he normally found comfort in observing the rules laid out for social interaction, he hadn't minded the few breaches of etiquette that evening. Chaswick and his wife were more than affable, as had been their guests.

Collette, however, presented something of a conundrum.

She fit, and yet she didn't.

Throughout the evening, he'd found his gaze landing on her more than was strictly proper. She dressed like a lady, she carried herself like a lady, she even spoke like a lady. But there was something in her eyes—a wariness. One he recognized because he'd seen it before in his brother.

As a youth, Addison had considered Rowan an equal member of their family, perhaps more than equal since he was older, and deserving of all the same rights and privileges bestowed upon himself. But at the age of six, when a tutor had been hired for the sole purpose of preparing Addison to one day become the duke, the relationship between the two brothers took a subtle shift.

Because Rowan had no need of such training.

When his tutor had refused to provide Addison with an adequate explanation for that, he had taken his questions to his father. The answers provided that day went on to shape much of his later outlook on life.

ANNABELLE ANDERS

His father had explained that Rowan was a bastard, and as much as he'd like his older son to be his heir, it simply was not possible.

"Why can't Rowan be your heir?" Addison had asked.

"Because I didn't marry his mother."

"Why not?"

"There are two categories of women, son." It was rare for his father to shower such undivided attention on him, so, even at such a young age, Addison had taken careful note of his father's words.

"Marriageable and unmarriageable." His father had explained that Rowan's mother fell into the second category. "As a duke, as a man with honor, if you compromise a woman who falls in the first category, you must marry her. But if you compromise a woman who falls in the second category, you must not. It's a matter of honor."

Untarnished debutantes from established, distinguished families were top of the marriageable list. Farther down were respectable widows and heiresses, and lastly came gently bred females forced to act as teachers, chaperones, and governesses.

The second category encompassed everyone else, beginning with debutantes with besmirched reputations, disreputable widows, illegitimates, middle class, and—it went without saying—dancers, courtesans, and prostitutes.

Miss Jones, as Addison saw her, fell into the first category. He'd not considered before that she also fell into the second one.

He'd not truly comprehended her reasons for refusing his proposal. He had heard them, but not listened. If he had, he might have already surmised that as far as she was concerned, she believed herself to be wholly in the unmarriageable category.

Rowan had realized this about her. Of course, he had.

So why did Addison feel a persistent need to treat her as though she was in the first? Was it because his desire to marry her had more to do with the woman herself than the circumstances of her birth?

Because in being honest with himself, honor was no longer the only thing compelling him to get her to the altar.

"I'm taking a young woman driving tomorrow afternoon, Brown. Please inform Tibbs to have the curricle ready at fifty minutes past one."

"I hadn't realized any suitable young ladies were residing in town just now," his manservant commented. "One of the ladies on your mother's list, by chance?"

"God, no." Addison exhaled. Of all the uncertainties surrounding Miss Jones, he was in no doubt that his mother would not approve of her. She tended to see matters in black and white.

As his father had. And his grandfather before him.

Addison bid his valet good night, extinguished the last remaining candles, and climbed into bed. He would see her tomorrow. He would drive her to one of the more private sections of the park. He would discover whether that kiss had been an anomaly.

∾

"THE DUKE OF BEDWELL is taking you driving?" Bethany paused in spreading the jam on her morning toast to pin a questioning gaze on Collette.

"He's likely showing his appreciation for her efforts with

his sister. They do have a prior association, darling." Chase said, hardly pausing before taking another bite of bacon, while Collette squirmed beneath her sister-in-law's all too knowing gaze.

"The duke's sister was one of my top students in the few days I spent at Miss Primm's. He was in need of reassurance that the school is the best place for her." Collette picked at the egg on her plate. She was nervous for the day, and whenever she was nervous, her appetite went into hiding.

"I'm not certain that school is an appropriate place for any young woman of character," Chase added. "Not while Primm bows to the wishes of the likes of that Metcalf woman." It was a sore spot for him, and Collette appreciated his loyalty.

"She didn't have much choice," Collette gently reminded him. "And Miss Shipley wrote me an excellent reference. She said neither she nor Miss Primm were happy about letting me go, but they stood to lose nearly half their students otherwise."

"Not sure I'd count those sorts of students a loss," he grumbled.

"Chase." Bethany placed her hand on his. "It's not fair to blame the girls for their parents' actions. That's twenty girls whose lives would have been uprooted." But then she smiled. "And speaking of uprooting lives, Chase has agreed to take me down to Brighton for a short holiday before winter sets in. We're going to be leaving tomorrow."

A look of adoration passed between her brother and his wife. It was almost as though he knew her secret already. Bethany flushed and raised her toast to her lips.

Collette wouldn't be surprised if Bethany had told him

the night before. She doubted they kept anything from one another very long.

What would it be like to have someone like that in her life? Her father had loved her mother in his own way but not in that all-encompassing way her brother loved Bethany.

"When you go with the duke, you'll want to be sure to wear a bonnet. And a wool coat as well. When I ventured into the garden this morning, the winds were already picking up."

If the weather turned, the duke would have an excellent reason to cancel their appointment. Did she want that?

She didn't.

Because as unsettled as he made her feel, she also liked talking to him. She liked… him.

"I hope it doesn't rain," she said.

"It won't," Chase declared without looking up from his food. "The weather doesn't dare inconvenience dukes. Or so Blackheart would have me believe."

And just as her brother predicted, the storm held off.

Although the sky was gray and gloomy hours later, the streets remained dry, giving Collette every reason to expect her escort for the afternoon to present himself at the allotted time. Because of course, he would arrive precisely on the agreed upon hour, and she would be prepared to receive him.

Diana had once tried to convince her that it was a lady's responsibility to keep a man waiting, but doing so made no sense to Collette. It was disrespectful of his time, wasteful, rude, and inconsiderate.

Not to mention petty and silly.

So at two before two, Collette was already waiting in the

drawing room, gloves and bonnet ready on the sofa beside her. Bethany sat across from her, tugging at her embroidery.

And when the knock sounded, Collette was on her feet before Mr. Ingles could even open the door, sliding her hands into her gloves.

"My Lady." The duke stepped inside, bowed in Bethany's direction, and then turned to Collette. "Miss Jones." How did he manage to do that? Steal the air out of a room the minute he stepped into it?

"Your Grace." Bethany rose, sliding a chastising glance in Collette's direction that said something akin to, *'Don't be so eager.'* "We so enjoyed having your company last night. I hope you'll join us again soon."

Would Collette be in London the next time they invited him? An anxious feeling gripped her at the thought, and she fumbled when she went to tie the ribbons on her bonnet. It wasn't that she would regret missing dinner parties. She didn't belong really, anyhow. It was rather the all-around uncertainty that lurked in her future.

"I look forward to that as it was my pleasure." He turned his gaze on Collette. "You will want a coat."

"Right here." Mr. Ingles appeared behind her, holding her gray coat up so she could slide her arms inside. It was a coat that a teacher would wear.

Bethany grimaced, shaking her head, but refrained from suggesting Collette wear the prettier coat that had been delivered earlier that week.

With her bonnet finally tied, and her coat buttoned, Collette endured the exchange of a few more niceties between Bethany and the duke, and then allowed him to lead her outside and down the front steps.

Uncertain as to why he'd even suggested this outing, she

kept quiet for as long as she could, not bothering to attempt any conversation until she was seated beside him, high off the ground, in a vehicle that did not seem at all as though it had been designed to carry ladies.

"We may yet have rain today." An utterly foolish conversational gambit but also one that gave nothing away as to her nervousness. Perhaps that was why people so often discussed the weather. It prevented them from having to give anything of their emotions, their thoughts, or feelings away.

"It should hold off for our drive. Did you enjoy yourself last night?" Not as bland as her topic but only slightly more original.

She could feel him all along the side of her, much as she had when they'd sat on the stairs together.

"The guests were lovely. I always enjoy meeting Chase and Bethany's friends." Why did she sound so breathless?

"Are they not your friends as well?"

Collette stared down at his hands. He wore leather gloves and handled the two horses as though it was something he'd been doing all his life.

"They are not, really." She didn't think to answer him with anything other than the truth.

"Because your father was not married to your mother." Now he was being original.

"Yes."

"But not because any of them looked down on you. It's because of how you see yourself." She glanced sideways at him in surprise. When she'd reminded him that she'd not belonged before, he hadn't seemed to understand. Why did he now? She turned again to study him. Since he was intent upon the road ahead, she was able to study his profile, his determined jawline, lips that were not thin, nor too full, and a nose that, from the side, appeared far more ducal than it did from the front—rounded—and hooking down just slightly on the end.

"It's not how I see myself. It is who I am," she said.

"You are a sister, a teacher." He met her stare briefly before turning his attention back to the road. "A lady."

Oh, but was she?

"I am also a daughter," she rejoined. "Unacknowledged by her father."

"You would have been a different person, then, if your father had married your mother and acknowledged his daughters?"

"Of course not." But she immediately reconsidered her answer.

"Although it is my brother who, in fact, shares this sort of experience with you," he said, "you and I have more in common than one might think."

The vehicle lurched as he turned them off of the paved road and into the graveled one inside the park.

Her first inclination was to dismiss such a ridiculous statement as nonsense. But he was not joking.

"I can think of very little we share in common, Your Grace."

"The natural order of life has somehow failed us both," he said. They were leaving the tall houses and manicured gardens of Mayfair behind and disappearing into a large copse of trees. For as long as she'd known, this park had been within walking distance of her home. It was a place that catered to London's elite and yet she and her sisters had taken great pleasure in the wilderness of it.

She'd considered it her park, but had it ever been, really?

"Go on," she encouraged him, curious as to how the natural order of life could have possibly failed a duke.

"You ought to be living your life as the daughter of a baron. You ought to have been raised with like ladies and all due respect. You ought not to have been dismissed from your teaching position if that is how you wish to live your life." His throat moved, as though he was swallowing an unwanted emotion.

And then she understood.

"You ought to be living your life as the second son of a duke," she said. "Not as the duke."

He didn't respond but dipped his chin in agreement. "I accept the duties of the title, and I will do my best to bring honor to it. But by all rights, it belongs to my brother."

"But there is nothing to be done about it."

"No," he answered. "Not that my brother would accept it if there was." His mouth twisted into something that was part grimace, part grin, making Collette think she'd like to meet his brother someday.

"Are you the same person you would be if you were not the duke?" This was not at all the conversation she'd expected to have with him today—something philosophical but also personal. It was the sort of conversation she might have had with Diana, or Chase even.

Not with a duke.

"Outwardly, no. Inside, I think yes. I have found ways to keep that person alive."

For some reason, this answer made her heart swell. Because people were often so much more than what they showed to the world.

"How?" She didn't care if this was too personal of a question to ask him. It was he who had opened this subject up, after all.

He glanced behind them and seemed to make a decision. "I have something to show you." In a surprising move, he steered the two horses around in a half circle so that they were returning the way they'd come. "Fancy a trip to Bond Street?"

WHAT IF?

*T*his was not at all what Addison had intended for this drive, but talking to her—*getting to know her*—felt natural, *right*. And shockingly, he wanted her to know him, as well.

"Would you be a different person on the inside if your father had accepted you?" he asked once he had the horses headed toward the street again.

She was shaking her head, as though she would deny him an answer but also as though she was searching for one.

"I don't know," she said.

She was lying.

"You said I wasn't going to have to go to Scotland." She changed the subject before he could press her. "What did you mean by that?"

She'd done this on more than one occasion. Changed a subject or diverted a conversation. Normally, she'd done it out of impatience or curiosity. This time, she was deflecting.

Miss Jones most definitely did not fit squarely into any

one particular category he'd formed in his mind about women.

"I didn't mean to add to your worries when I told you that your brother had risked his social standing when he presented you and your sister to the *ton*." This had bothered him last night. He didn't want her to think he was manipulating her emotions in order to suit his purposes.

Because as it so happened, her guilt could be considered useful for him.

"I know," she said.

"I just wanted to give you an honest answer."

"I would expect nothing else from you. Even if it isn't something I particularly wish to hear."

"But as it so happens." He turned them onto the street and then steered around a slow-moving carriage. "I can help you with that."

"This is why you told me I wouldn't have to go to Scotland?" Her question wasn't really a question.

"Yes." He would have preferred to not be driving while having this discussion, but... "By marrying me, you will increase your brother's standing considerably."

Rowan's words niggled in his mind. She'd told him no once already. It ought to have fulfilled his duty to honor.

She sat silently. Perhaps she was coming around as she wasn't rejecting him outright.

His lungs seemed to squeeze inside his chest as the silence drew out.

Why am I pressing her on this?

"I was rather hoping you were going to offer me a teaching position." She sighed.

"If I could convince Fiona to leave school, I might have considered that an option. As it is, I have no need of a tutor."

"But... Do you actually wish to marry me or is this still because your honor compels you for kissing me that day?" Her question removed yet another barrier between the two of them. It made her vulnerable. It was raw and more than he'd expect from... anyone.

The kiss.

It was part of what compelled his proposal. The memory plagued him. He'd been taunted by the notion that he'd never experience another like it ever again.

She was not an unmarriageable woman, even if she was not completely marriageable. She didn't fit into his rules. She definitely would not fit into his mother's rules.

He moved the leather straps of the reins into his right hand and after a quick glance down, covered both of hers with his left, waiting to see if she would pull them away.

"A little of both," he answered, his heart skipping a beat.

She wanted his honesty.

An unfamiliar energy sparked between them. Not completely unfamiliar—no—but he'd only ever felt it with her.

The power of it affected more than one of his organs.

"What does that even mean?" Her voice came out tight-sounding.

He stroked his thumb over her softly-worn gloves and the energy hummed even louder.

"I want to marry you regardless. But that kiss, yes. It is part of my reason." Even in his own ears, he sounded like a lovesick fool. "Because I... rather enjoyed kissing you. Very much in fact. And I wish to do it again."

This was not at all what he'd set out to tell her today.

She turned to stare at him, as she did so, her hands

turned in his, embracing them. "Because you enjoyed...? You wish to...?"

Addison pulled the curricle to the side of the street, parking beneath a tree. The wind had picked up and a few leaves gusted around them.

He turned to meet her startled eyes and leaned forward. "I do."

And he kissed her.

∾

"Oh!" Collette parted her lips just as his mouth settled on hers.

Rather than answer her question, he was showing her.

His mouth felt cool and firm at first, from the wind. And he tasted like the outdoors, but also like the familiar spices she'd dreamt about more than once. He swept his tongue between her lips, softening his own at the same time.

"Oh." She'd not imagined how wonderful it had been. Was this kiss even better?

She squeezed his hand between hers. Her limbs were not melting simply because he was a duke. Her heart wasn't expanding simply because he was so very handsome and impressive.

All of these feelings were for him—the man—the person. Himself.

He palmed the back of her bonnet, tilting her head and deepening the kiss. If she wasn't already gripping his hand, she would have wound her arms around his neck.

What was closer than a kiss? Because that's what she wanted.

His mouth abandoned hers but just barely. He trailed it to the corner of her lips, and then along her jaw.

If not for the oncoming sound of another carriage, Collette likely would have turned and straddled him.

Instead, she jerked away, her heart racing in excitement and fear and something wholly unfamiliar.

He had just kissed her.

Again!

"My apologies." He looked as startled as she felt. "Does that answer your question?"

Today, his eyes were almost the exact color of the sky, the color of the approaching storm. His lips were shining and wet from... hers.

Otherwise, he looked as perfectly put together as when he'd arrived to collect her from her brother's townhouse.

Had his kiss answered her question, or had it only given rise to a slew of other ones?

When she didn't say anything, he calmly turned back to the horses and, using only one hand, he pulled them back onto the street.

His other hand remained clasped between hers.

He'd said he had liked their first kiss.

She'd liked it too. In fact, she'd secretly treasured it. But this kiss. It had been more deliberate, and he had not initiated it out of any sort of panic or fear.

She liked this one just as much... perhaps more.

"Did you enjoy the second kiss as much?" she asked. "Do you still wish for more?" Because it might have been something of a disappointment for him, since he had not been experiencing any sort of emotional distress at the time.

She felt him chuckle beside her. "Yes, to both of your questions."

Oh.

Something blossomed inside of her. He was able to touch her with his words the same as with a kiss.

If he hadn't already expressed his desire to marry her, then she would suspect he wanted to set her up as a mistress. Was this how her father had made her mother feel? Because Collette wasn't sure she could turn the duke down if that was what he wanted.

And after only two kisses, she'd nearly forgotten her own name.

She released his hand when he turned onto Bond Street where the traffic was heavier. After driving a short distance, he pulled to a halt outside of a bookstore. He climbed down first, leaving her perched atop the tall contraption while he tossed a coin to a lad, presumably to keep watch of the horses and vehicle, and then circled around to assist her down.

"You can place one foot there." He indicated one of the spokes on the large wheel. "Don't worry, I've got you."

When his hands settled on her waist, she smiled. This could very well be why a gentleman might take a lady driving in such a tall vehicle.

Because she was utterly at his mercy and didn't mind it in the slightest when he slowly lowered her onto the ground. And if she was not mistaken, his hands lingered longer than was necessary.

"You wished to show me something in the bookstore?" She did her best to act normal, happy that her brain was able to put words together properly again. Even so, her voice sounded breathless in her own ears.

"I do." A light in his eyes made him seem as though a weight had lifted off his shoulders. Because he'd kissed her?

Or because of something else? "This way." He hooked his arm for her to take and then covered her fingertips with his free hand, briefly, making her feel... protected as they entered the store.

As this was the nearest bookseller to her own home, she'd visited it on numerous occasions.

"Are we looking for anything in particular?" she asked, eyeing the row that held her favorites, mysteries and murders made even more interesting by a good romantic storyline. He too, apparently had visited before and led her deeper into the store, past the mysteries, past the biographies.

"You asked me," he spoke softly, halting between two long shelves in what she believed were adventure stories, "how I kept my true self alive—the man inside—the part of me who is not Bedwell."

She nodded, noticing his fingers twisting a ring on his opposite hand. Also appreciating how lovely those hands were. Capable looking, but also... elegant. Much like him.

He must have a favorite book for when he felt disconnected from who he was on the inside, from the essence that was uniquely him.

She had a few of those as well.

Exhaling a deep breath, he reached around her to pluck a thick, dark red leather book off the shelf. Without a word, he stared down at it, rubbing his thumb along the embossed writing.

And then offered it to her.

Collette read the title, turned it over, and then opened it to the first few pages.

The Crossing, by Holden Hampden. Published by Smythe, Smythe and Tufts Publishing House, London, 1828.

Ch. One.

Angus closed his eyes, allowing the gusts of sea mist to whip against his face, tossing his hair in every direction...

Collette lifted her gaze to his. "You wish to travel, to explore?"

"The wind could be harnessed," he said, "but never controlled, never bested, never enslaved even though sailors dreamed they could."

She dropped her stare back to the written words. He'd recited them, almost as though they were his own—"

"You wrote this," she whispered.

Because, of course, he would keep this secret. Who else knew? "You wrote a book?" But when she turned to examine the shelf, she realized she'd underestimated him. Standing adjacent to the empty space left by *The Crossing*, were several others, all bound in the same dark red leather but with different titles.

Spinning back around, she hugged the book to her chest.

He glanced down but then raised his gaze to meet hers again.

A lump of emotion formed in her throat. "You are *Holden Hampden?*"

He nodded, and then shrugged, still looking sheepish.

"Does anyone else know?"

"Rowan, my brother."

She turned to the shelf again, this time to drag her fingertips along the line of books. Six, in all. The distinct aroma of leather and paper permeated her senses.

"Anonymously," she guessed.

"Not even the publishers know."

Speechless, she pressed one hand flat against her chest.

He'd written books! Books that had been published by a

legitimate publishing house—a publishing house who had no idea that they were distributing stories written by one of England's very own dukes.

She'd yet to realize the depths of this man's character, but the more she got to know him, the more she wanted to explore them. What other fears did he have? What dreams taunted him? How did he see the world?

How did he see her?

The door clanged from the front as another customer entered.

"I would feel as though I belong." The words gushed out of her. She'd told him she didn't know what would be different about her if her father had married her mother, but she'd simply been afraid to admit it.

He looked confused for a moment.

"You asked me—"

"What would be different about you."

"Yes."

He dragged his fingertips slowly from her shoulder to cover her hand—where it rested on her heart. "The heart wants to belong." They might as well have been the only two people in the world. The air surrounding them was thick, preventing other souls from entering. "Sometimes," he smiled sadly, "the brain doesn't allow it."

"I know." Her voice caught.

"If belonging is a state of mind, Collette, we need to alter your thinking."

She exhaled a sound that wasn't a word nor was it a sob. It was an exclamation of utter confusion.

"Don't give me your answer yet. But promise me one thing."

Even though she knew better than ever to promise

something without knowing what it was, she found herself inexplicably agreeing to it. "Yes."

"Three things, actually."

"Very well." She smiled at this.

"Firstly, that you will not try to make up reasons not to marry me."

She nodded.

"Secondly, that you will not make plans to travel to Scotland. It would be rather inconvenient for me to have to chase after you for an answer."

She shook her head at this but answered, "I won't."

"And thirdly…" He tilted his head. "When we're together, in private, will you call me Addison?"

Which meant he intended to meet with her in private again. Was he courting her? He said he would wait for her answer.

"Not Holden?" she asked.

He grimaced. "My middle name."

Addison Holden Brierton. It was a lovely name. Perhaps the loveliest she'd ever heard for a man.

"So long as you will call me Collette." But he had already.

"Collette." Was the air even heavier?

"Addison." Such a lovely name. "Will you promise me…?"

"Yes?"

To kiss me again. But she could not say that. Feeling heat flood up her neck and into her cheeks, she shook her head and then licked her lips.

He grinned. "You can count on it."

TO FULMINATE

fter visiting the bookstore, he took her to a tea house where she asked him all sorts of questions about writing, which led to a discussion about words and their power, and he, in turn, asked her questions about Latin.

"A single word by itself can paint a picture—knowing the precise, comprehensive meaning of any one word truly enhances communication." She found herself telling him some of what she'd told her students.

"Tell me one of your favorites." His attentiveness drew out more excitement than she usually showed anyone.

"*Fulminare.* It literally means *to flash with thunderbolts.* Picture a ferocious storm in your mind. Now, take the word *fulminate.* One English definition is *to vehemently protest.* In Italian, it means *to strike dead.* Metamorphically, it was used by the church when referring to a formal condemnation." Which, she imagined in those days, could result in tragic consequences.

"It's violent."

"Not just yelling or arguing." She shook her head.

One corner of his mouth twitched up as he leaned forward.

Both of them rested their hands on the table and he slid his forward, barely brushing his fingers against hers. "Do you fulminate often?"

It was a silly question for him to ask. "Only with Diana."

They shared a few stories about each of their siblings, and time flew by much too quickly.

"I'd best return you to your brother's house or he'll come after me with a pistol." He glanced at his watch and winced.

"He won't." Would he? It was only a trip to a bookstore.

Since she'd not brought along her reticule, she'd lacked funds to purchase the first of Addison's books but vowed to return the very next day for just that purpose. She didn't care if it cost her an entire month of the salary she'd set aside from Miss Primm's. She was determined to have a glimpse into his thoughts.

A slow drizzle began to fall just as the horses pulled them up to her brother's house. This time when she waited for the duke—for *Addison*—to come around and assist her to the ground, she did so with a heightened sense of anticipation.

He couldn't kiss her again—not on her brother's doorstep. He should not have kissed her earlier, and they'd been lucky not to have been seen. Had it been springtime rather than autumn, Mayfair would be buzzing with society and their indiscretion would have already made its way through all the gossips.

"We were lucky to have escaped most of this." Addison's gaze shot to the sky and then back to her as he settled his hands on her waist. She took hold of his shoulders, trusting that he would lower her safely to the walk.

The moment reminded her of some she'd seen between Bethany and Chase—which was wonderful but also a little terrifying.

"Thank you." She exhaled when her feet touched the ground. The drizzle chose that moment to strengthen to more of a downpour and yet he didn't release her, nor did she move to rush inside.

"Thank you for allowing me to drive you, and for humoring my ramblings about my little hobby."

"Not at all. I was honored that you showed me." She blinked away a few drops of water as she stared up at him, her hands still on his shoulders. "You won't mind, will you? If I read one of them?"

"Please, don't think you must." He was shaking his head, looking sheepish all over again. "Just the ramblings of a foolish man."

A man. Not of a duke. "Not foolish." He was staring at her mouth, and she flicked her gaze at his. She'd never wanted anything as much in her life as she wanted him to kiss her again. The longing was a physical ache, one that very nearly had her reaching onto her toes and tugging his head down to hers.

"Ahem." The voice from the house had her dropping her hands and pushing away from heaven. Because that's what it felt like to be in his arms. She'd later mock herself for such romantic thoughts but for now had something altogether less pleasant to deal with.

Addison dragged his gaze away from her to meet that of the scowling person standing on the doorstep.

Chase.

Rain pounding on his head, her brother stood just outside the door, coatless, wearing rolled-up shirtsleeves, elegant trousers, and only stockings on his feet.

"Inside." He addressed Collette with a jerk of the head.

Casting a reluctant parting glance at the duke, she was unable to meet his eyes since he was glaring back at her brother. She ducked her head and rushed inside. Maneuvering around Chase, she was surprised she wasn't dry the moment she stepped inside, so hot was the anger rolling off her brother.

Bethany awaited her in the foyer and, wincing, dropped a blanket around Collette's shoulders. "He was just going to come looking for you."

"But I was perfectly safe."

"You were alone with him for hours."

And if it had been up to Collette, she would have sat talking with Addison even longer. "I'm sorry—" A tremor from the cold ran through her. Either from the cold, or from guilt, or fear of what her brother intended to do.

Or perhaps from the combination of all of those.

"Come into the drawing room and sit by the fire." Bethany shot a concerned glance toward the door but led Collette up the stairs anyway. "What was Bedwell thinking? Keeping you out so long? This is all my fault. I shouldn't have allowed you to go with him. Not after I saw that look—"

"After you saw what look?" Collette halted inside the door while Bethany toed the ottoman closer to the fire. Collette didn't remember any particular look.

"Right after he offered Lady Sheffield his arm, he glanced over his shoulder at Sir Grimsley. And... it's hard to describe but... Oh, Collette, I should have realized. Here, come inside and sit down." But she herself crossed to the window, her fingertips rapidly tapping her thumb one by one. "They have not come to blows," she announced as she shamelessly watched the two men below.

Good Lord! Collette dropped onto the cushioned bench and huddled beneath the blanket. "I didn't think. We were just talking…"

"It didn't look like talking from here." Bethany slid her a glance but then, just as quickly, stared out the window again. "Good thing it's raining, or the neighbors would certainly be getting an earful. At the same time, I can't hear what's being said either."

"What are they doing now?" Collette buried her face in her hands. She had known she had sat with Addison for longer than was strictly appropriate, but she'd done nothing wrong. Had she?

"Your duke is looking quite formidable. He isn't doing much talking. Oh, wait, he's nodding now. They are in agreement about something." Bethany rushed away from the window and sat down in her normal spot just as the opening and closing of a door sounded from downstairs in the foyer.

Seconds later, her brother appeared, his hair streaming around his face, his clothing sopping, with water dripping onto the shining wooden floor.

"A bloody duke, Collette?"

But Bethany had shot off the settee again and was settling a blanket around her husband's shoulders.

"We can discuss this later, Chase. Come upstairs and change into something dry. Collette, you need to get out of that wet gown as well."

But Collette didn't move right away. "We went to the

Opus Emporium, and then a teahouse. All we did was talk." Except for in those moments when he'd pulled his vehicle to the side of the road.

"Be prepared to receive him first thing tomorrow morning." Chase spoke through clenched teeth. And with that, her amiable, compassionate brother spun around and marched out of the room.

Bethany glanced back at Collette. "I need to calm him down. Will you be all right if I—"

"Yes." But Collette slumped even lower where she sat at the hearth.

"Everything is going to work out fine. His temper won't last long, and we'll work everything out over dinner. Come upstairs as well. Polly can draw you a hot bath, and I promise you'll feel much better after."

Collette rose and then nearly stumbled over her own feet as she drifted toward the door. She knew she was in some sort of scrape, but she didn't completely understand why.

The rules that these people lived by—they felt like a difficult maze where each turn had her more confused than before.

All she knew was that she'd never seen her brother so angry, not even after Lord Greystone had compromised Diana—which wasn't really fair at all—seeing as Diana's indiscretions hadn't been nearly as innocent as Collette's...

Be prepared to receive him first thing tomorrow morning.

Had she finally run out of choices? And if she had, shouldn't she be more disappointed at that realization?

TRAPPED WITH THE DUKE

"I HAVEN'T SEEN a storm like this all year." Mr. Brown observed.

Addison closed his eyes and relished the feel of the hot water his valet poured over his head. Having spent an additional half an hour driving around in the rain, he had returned soaking wet, and although he ought to be chilled to the bone, Addison's blood flowed warm enough.

One would expect to feel defensive upon being blasted by Collette's brother like that, but Addison rather respected the man for it. He would have done no less if the tables had been turned.

Chaswick was a good man and an excellent brother.

What the devil had caused him to act so very out of character? Something about being in her company shattered his normal reservations. He'd experienced it that day in the stairwell, and then again, in her classroom. Talking with her at the dinner party, he'd wanted to experience it again.

Whatever "it" was.

Today, he'd intended to keep her out for forty-five minutes, certainly no more than an hour. And he'd intended to present her with all the logical reasons she needed to marry him. If she had refused, he would have made inquiries for her as to suitable employment closer to London. Close enough, at least, that she could make somewhat frequent visits to see her family.

His plans had gone awry.

Addison accepted the soap from Brown and went to scrubbing himself thoroughly. His skin was cold to the touch, but beneath it he was hot, jumpy. And whenever he remembered the kiss, lusty as hell.

"Leave me," he instructed his valet. He'd have a warm soak and do some writing later this evening.

"Very good, sir. A towel and banyan are hanging over the chair."

Lightning flashed as the door closed and thunder cracked the air three seconds later. *Fulminatus*. He grinned. How very appropriate.

Addison slid down in the tub, submerging his entire head and holding himself there until he had no choice but to emerge for air.

He ought to have been considerably more discreet about the location he'd chosen to kiss her. Anywhere would have been better than sitting atop his curricle parked on the side of Curzon Street.

He might have chosen somewhere he could do more than kiss her, while at the same time ensuring neither of them fell off the damn bench.

Instinctively, he wound his hand around his cock, thick and hard from nothing more than the memory of a kiss.

What was it about her?

He tilted his head back, his hand slick from the soap, making it easy to slide up and down his length.

When he'd first come of age, he'd taken advantage of his position and resources by setting up a mistress, much as his peers had done. Daphne Dubois—likely not even her given name, but he'd enjoyed her. He'd liked her. He'd not enjoyed the sordid nature of it all. In the years since he'd let her go, his encounters had been brief, spontaneous, and, since he was also selective, quite limited.

Collette was unlike any woman he'd ever known. Unbridled by a proper upbringing, she spoke her mind. And yet she was a lady.

When he'd assisted her off the curricle, he'd been tantalized by the curve of her hip—a gentle slope formed with mostly taut flesh.

What would her skin feel like beneath his hands? Silky? Satiny?

The image of wide-open indigo eyes, staring up at him, hiding nothing of her own desire, edged him closer.

Addison.

His given name on her lips was an aphrodisiac in itself—lips that were pink and plump.

He imagined her unclothed, her breasts in his palms, her smooth back pressed against his chest while his cock throbbed between her legs. And those little breathy sounds she'd made when he'd nipped at the corner of her mouth. He'd taste that place on her neck where her pulse fluttered beneath tender skin, and then latch onto it, claiming her. He would lose himself in her heat as he moved in and out, penetrating deeper with each stroke.

So good. Her inner muscles would grip him tightly. She would be hot and wet. Gentle splashing sounds barely met Addison's consciousness as he worked himself harder, eyes closed. She was riding him as he nipped at her breasts. She was so damned beautiful.

He jerked and held his breath when the inevitable lighting shot down his spine, killing him but also filling a void, making him whole and breaking him into a thousand pieces at the same time.

Seconds passed in which he returned to his surroundings, hearing the rain pouring on the window and aware the water in the copper tub had grown cold.

Climbing out, one hand braced against the wall, Addison didn't dismiss the images of her that lingered in his mind.

ANNABELLE ANDERS

He ran the towel over his shoulders, down his arms. He'd told Rowan she was beautiful, but there was more to her than that.

Her eyes, which were a normal shade of blue and ought to be nothing out of the ordinary, succeeded in pulling him directly into her thoughts. He had no power against the curiosity she evoked—when he was with her, they explored unexpected ideas and subjects in ways he'd never considered before.

And the crux of it was he liked taking these unexpected detours.

With her.

Upon their initial meeting, he'd taken one look at her pinched lips and deemed her to be an uninteresting teacher. After she'd loosed them, he'd added annoying to that description.

When had he become captivated by that same mouth?

If he hadn't just found his rather reprehensible release, he might have been tempted to summon other scenarios for it. Instead, he slipped his arms into his banyan and opened the door.

"Do you wish to dress for dinner, Your Grace?" Brown stood at the ready, looking perfectly proper but all too knowing, damn him.

Addison grimaced. "Not tonight." He'd be dining alone. On many occasions, he'd sat unaccompanied, wearing formal evening wear, and allowed his staff to serve him with all pomp and circumstances. But only when he was going out afterward.

He'd made no social commitments for that evening.

"I've business to attend to in my study."

"No jacket then, I'll lay out your maroon dressing gown."

"Yes." Addison would attempt to shelve concerns over the turn his life would be taking tomorrow morning by adding a chapter or two to his latest book. It seemed to be the one thing in this world that made sense in his life.

Even though it didn't, really.

THE DUKE IS WAITING FOR MISS JONES

*A*lthough Collette was dressed and ready for dinner, she hovered in her chamber, delaying more reprimands Chase no doubt had ready to heap on her.

Not that he would be in the wrong, but his expressions of disappointment alone, would provide more than enough punishment for her carelessness.

He wouldn't yell but he would stare at her with those eyes, so very like their father's, and give her that *look*. The look he'd had when he'd found her hiding behind a potted plant at her first ball and when she'd refused to meet with a prospective suitor.

Considering his earlier mood, tonight could very well prove to be far worse than either of those.

She jumped when a knock sounded but wasn't surprised to see Bethany's head peek around the door when it opened. "I thought you might be dallying in here."

Her sister-in-law drifted in, looking unusually pretty in a kelly-green gown with blue embroidery around the bodice.

Collette exhaled. "You're coming to know me all too well."

Bethany dropped onto a tall-backed chair and smiled weakly. "You rather remind me of myself sometimes."

"I do?" Bethany was the eldest daughter of an earl—an acknowledged and *legitimate* daughter of an earl.

"I still don't quite understand it myself, but I could never really imagine the man I loved choosing me for his wife. For different reasons than yours, I suppose."

"Chase couldn't have found a better person to spend his life with." Collette meant it. "He's happier than I've ever known him to be."

"Ah, but, neither of us planned any of this. It just sort of… happened."

Collette nodded. Bethany nor her brother had ever told her the precise details of their rushed marriage. They hadn't needed to. Collette had read of it in the papers.

It was a miracle Chase hadn't been banned from England forever.

"Do you like the duke?" Bethany asked.

"I do. But he's a duke." She was shaking her head.

"He's going to offer for you in the morning. He was about to kiss you when Chase found the two of you outside. Even if he hadn't been, he'd kept you away for nearly four hours—without a chaperone."

"I can't marry him, Bethany. He's a *duke*—as in, superseded by only princes and kings," Collette explained, as though Bethany had not quite digested this particular fact.

"And you are a lady."

"But not really," Collette argued.

"You are. And the sooner you come to accept this, the sooner you can go about living your life. From the day I met you, I felt an affinity with you for this. Because as long as you are convinced you are undeserving, others will see you that way too."

"But my father—"

"Fathers are funny things, Collette, in how they shape the way we see ourselves. Trust me when I tell you that I allowed my father—my family—to dictate the way I saw myself for years. I felt trapped because of their expectations. It was only after I looked within myself that I met the person I was meant to be."

Collette blinked as she tried to absorb Bethany's words. It felt impossible to imagine seeing herself as anyone other than who she was. As hard as she tried to move her perspective, it refused to budge.

Because nothing in the world could ever make her legitimate, and if the people of the *Ton* couldn't forget this, how could she?

Bethany's smile was sad. "What are you going to do?"

Collette pictured Addison standing before her in the bookstore, looking proud and yet tentative at the same time. And later, asking her questions, and listening to her opinions and sharing his. Talking with him had felt both natural and invigorating.

And then of course, there had been the kiss in the stairwell, on the curricle, and the almost kiss on Chase's front step.

Warmth blossomed and spread from her heart to her toes and fingertips.

"I do like him," she admitted.

Bethany's brows rose.

"I only wish he wasn't a duke."

"But...?" Bethany tilted her head, patiently watching Collette struggle to find some sort of answer.

"I can't be a duchess. My mother was my father's mistress! People will speculate the very worst and I would be the laughingstock of Mayfair. And what would people say about him? Besides, I know nothing about duchessing, I wouldn't even know where to begin."

"All legitimate concerns," Bethany agreed, when Collette had secretly been hoping her sister-in-law would try to convince her otherwise. Aside from that, the word legitimate never failed to make Collette squirm. "And although there isn't anything you could do about the opinions of others, I'm sure you could learn the actual duchessing part —that is if his mother is willing to help you."

"She will hate me." Collette sighed. Marrying him would be a nightmare. An exciting, romantic nightmare.

"She might." Bethany truly wasn't mincing her words tonight. "I've never met her and it's possible she'd object to you for all the same reasons you are reluctant."

That part actually did sound like a nightmare.

"But, Collette, the choice won't be hers to make—not if he keeps his promise to Chase, which I've no doubt he will. And the decision will be between you and Bedwell. If you can somehow see a way to happiness with him, what have you got to lose?"

Which was, for certain, a valid question.

She'd lost her position at the school and her sisters had all gone their separate ways. The choices she was left with were hardly the ones she'd dreamed of.

Collette grimaced. "If I fail at duchessing, will you allow me to live with you as your children's favorite aunt?" It was a silly question, really. Because she doubted duchesses who couldn't uphold the dignity of their position could do anything other than hide away in the country.

"If I didn't send you packing for hiding in the loo for most of the Ravensdale's ball last spring, I doubt there's anything I'd turn you away for. But speaking of children…" Her entire demeanor transformed to one of… pure joy. "Chase knows. He said he suspected." Bethany grinned. "But he couldn't stop smiling. I never thought I could be so happy—and terrified—at the same time."

"This is wonderful!" Collette was not surprised that Chase had suspected. There was just something different about Bethany lately—a dewy, dreamy look. It was subtle, but if she'd recognized it, her brother certainly had as well. "I thought you were going to wait though. When did you tell him?"

"Just this afternoon. I thought it as good of time as any and it did manage to take his mind off of throttling a certain sister." She smirked. "Or challenging a duke."

The possibility of her brother and Addison meeting on a field of honor was a horrific one. "I'm so sorry! I didn't mean to cause trouble."

Bethany waved a hand. "It's not as bad as it seems. And Chase knows he's not allowed to duel again without my permission—not after what happened last spring."

"I should just leave London tonight—travel to Easter Park and stay with Sarah and my mother." Because she did not want to go to Scotland. She loved her family too much to martyr herself that way. She needed her family. And not just Chase and Bethany, but Sarah and Diana and her mother.

She never felt uncomfortable about who she was when she was with them.

Also, she'd promised Addison she wouldn't go to Scotland.

"We all cause trouble at some time or another. Apparently, it's your season." Bethany grinned and then grew serious again. "You don't have to give him your answer right away. If you think waiting will help, ask for a week, or longer. Because marrying him will change everything. And those changes are for life. If you hate it, you'll be trapped with the duke forever, but there is always the possibility…"

"Of what?" Collette insisted.

"That marrying him, that being with a man who loves you, and one you love in return, frees you to be the person you've always been meant to be."

But Collette didn't love the duke, and of course, he didn't love her.

They barely knew one another.

Even if she did rather enjoy kissing him and he'd said he enjoyed kissing her as well.

Was it possible it was the beginning of more than just that? Was it possible it was the beginning of love?

~

"YOU'RE UP EARLY." Chase glanced up from the plate filled with eggs and kidneys and more than one of Cook's buttery yeast buns. "I expect Bedwell any minute. You'll want to make yourself scarce until I give him permission to present his offer to you."

Collette nearly rolled her eyes at the absurdity of it all. The duke had already presented his offer on more than one occasion, and she'd declined him. Despite her discussion with Bethany, she hadn't changed her mind.

She could not accept.

She wasn't fit to be a duchess, so she would tell him no.

Her heart squeezed and then her stomach lurched when one of the attending manservants leaned over her shoulder to refill her cup. Tea was all she was going to be able to manage until this was over.

And then what?

"Did you sleep at all?" Bethany asked, averting her face away from her husband's plate to nibble on the single piece of toast on her own.

"Some," Collette lied.

"Collette, I've made a decision." Chase leaned back, glanced at Bethany, and when she nodded in encouragement, turned his attention back to her. "I should have arranged for formal training on etiquette and manners long before setting you and Diana loose on the ton. I was negligent not to have, and I consider myself lucky that Greystone did the honorable thing."

"He had no choice, he fell madly in love with Diana," Bethany reminded him.

"He had a choice for certain, and if he hadn't made the right one…" His gaze landed on Bethany. "Nonetheless, I've made arrangements with the Barnaby agency to send over a suitable instructor today. Collette, your lessons begin at one this afternoon."

"Regardless of what I decide?"

"*Especially* if you accept Bedwell's offer. You'll thank me later, trust me." Chase tore into one of the buns.

"You didn't think to ask me first?" Collette scowled. She wouldn't require etiquette lessons in the country with her mother and Sarah, nor did she think she'd need them if she had decided to take the position in Scotland. Chase might very well be one of her favorite people in the world but there were times, like this, when his arrogance unfortunately, resembled their father's all too clearly.

If he'd asked her rather than make such a decision on his own, she might have found the gesture to be sweet and considerate. Before she could argue further, however, the conversation was interrupted.

"Excuse me, My Lord," Mr. Ingles was standing in the doorway, hands behind his back. "The Duke of Bedwell has arrived. Would you like me to have him wait in the front drawing room, or--?"

"No. I'll meet with him in my study now." Chase took one last bite and was already pushing his chair back. He shot a glance at Collette. "I'll send for you shortly."

The earnest concern on her brother's face had her forgetting her irritation with him and brought stinging to her eyes. "I'm sorry," she muttered. "For making so much trouble."

"No more trouble than you're allotted." And with a wink, he disappeared, leaving Bethany and Collette sitting quietly, in a sort of resolved silence.

"Have you decided?" Bethany asked at last.

Collette recalled the duchesses who had been pointed out to her at the few balls she'd attended last spring. The Duchess of Cortland had been a dainty woman who appeared almost ethereal with eyes that were almost gold and blond hair so light it was practically white.

The other duchess, the Duchess of Montford, wasn't nearly as beautiful but the look in her eyes was one of dignity and grace. She'd had a faraway look in her eyes, making Collette believe she existed in a realm above them all.

Both ladies had obviously been comfortable in the knowledge that nothing they did would ever be judged or dismissed or looked down upon.

Impossible.

"Collette?" Bethany pressed. "Have you?"

"I'm going to decline," she said. "I'm not... I'll never be..."

"Oh." Her sister-in-law frowned. "So you don't like him then? You don't believe you could ever love him?"

"It's not that."

Bethany's frown deepened. "Then you are afraid."

Collette didn't bother denying the truth of that. "Terrified."

"And it doesn't bother you?"

"What doesn't bother me?"

"The fact that you might be making a mistake because you are willing to allow fear to dictate your decision?"

At such an accusation, Collette placed her cup back on the saucer, stunned into silence. Where was the supportive woman who'd encouraged her the night before?

For several minutes after that, the only sound in the room was that of Bethany nibbling at her toast.

Impossible. Marrying him was impossible.

"Miss Jones." Mr. Ingles returned, breaking the uncomfortable silence. "The duke is waiting for you."

Collette's stare caught and held Bethany's as panic flew through her.

Panic and excitement.

He had come. Tingles danced down her spine and released a flock of butterflies to tear around inside of her.

"Choose wisely." Bethany's eyes danced. She was being no help at all.

Collette rose as the footman who'd been attending the hot plates on the sideboard slid her chair backward.

"Collette." Chase was at the door now, his eyes focused and serious. "Don't do something you don't want to do. We're here for you regardless."

He stepped forward, grasped her arms, and dropped a soft kiss on her cheek.

"I know," she muttered, near tears. "I know."

And then, rolling her shoulders, she strolled out the door to where a duke waited to offer for her.

A duke, waiting for *her*, Collette Jones. It was almost laughable.

But when she opened the door, she wasn't laughing at all. Because she didn't see a duke pacing back and forth across the decorative rug, all she saw was Addison.

A CHANGE OF HEART

"Good morning." Collette swallowed hard as Ingles pulled the large double doors closed behind her. And then her stomach lurched. Because the inscrutable look in Addison's eyes nearly overwhelmed the warmth she saw, reminding her that although this was the same man from yesterday, he was also very much a duke.

She darted her gaze away from him, toward the windows that lined one of the walls. "I doubt we'll see more rain today." Oh, yes. She was coming to quite appreciate this weatherly topic for conversation. For the second time in as many days, meteorological commentary was saving her from saying something utterly nonsensical.

One side of his mouth quirked up. "The streets were washed clean in yesterday's torrent."

"And the air." She nodded.

"And the air," he agreed.

Excellent. They were making excellent progress. "Makes one appreciate a good roof," she added.

This time, she was certain she caught his chest shaking a little. "Indeed, along with a sound foundation."

She twisted her hands together. Perhaps Chase's idea to hire a tutor wasn't such a bad idea after all. She only wished she'd had a lesson on handling proposals *before* Addison arrived.

More specifically, on how one went about declining one. She'd experienced little success with her prior refusals.

"Won't you... sit down?" She remembered just in time that a gentleman wouldn't sit until she was seated and lowered herself onto the edge of the nearest settee.

He chose to sit on the opposite end and turned his legs so he was mostly facing her.

"You didn't catch cold from the rain yesterday?" He was very good at not showing any emotion in his expression. Did he resent being here? Was he even now, this very moment, berating himself for having kept her away from home for so long?

"Oh, no." Whether he resented the situation or not didn't matter anyway. "I was more worried that you would. What with standing in it listening to my brother go on and on and then having to drive yourself home." He was the same man she'd spent hours conversing with the day before and yet everything seemed different now. "I hope you indulged in a long hot bath when you arrived home."

An unusual expression flickered across his face. "Indeed."

"I'm glad. One mustn't be too careful with his or her health, and I'd never forgive myself if you were to take ill." And that was true. Because if she hadn't talked his ears off over their long, rather drawn-out tea, they would have not only returned before Chase became upset, but they also would have missed the rain altogether.

And despite his *dukishness*… he had become somewhat… dear to her.

"Did you work on your book last night?" He'd been struggling with a particular passage. It was one of the things they'd gotten caught up talking about. A new idea he'd had.

His gaze met hers in surprise. "I did, in fact. Two chapters, they're rough, as they always are, but I'm happy with what I have so far."

"I'm glad." She stared into his gray eyes, which seemed to have warmed, and in that moment found herself feeling all the emotions she'd felt yesterday, sitting atop his ridiculously tall vehicle and discussing kissing.

"But I haven't come here today to discuss my writing." He edged closer to her, flicking a glance toward the closed door as he did so. "Your brother told you to expect me?"

"He did." And her brother had expected him to make her an offer. "But—"

"I didn't do it intentionally—keep you out like that. It was reckless on my part, and Chaswick had every right to call me out for it. I hope you'll accept my apology." Even while apologizing, he appeared proud.

But his jaw ticked as though he was holding something back, and he was twisting the ring on his finger again. Was it possible he was nervous to speak with her today? It didn't really make sense. She tilted her head. "You are sorry then? That we spent the afternoon together?"

"Not at all." His eyes widened at that. "But I never intended to keep you so late. I should have realized." His jaw ticked again and then he exhaled and ran a hand through his hair. "I did realize. I was just being selfish."

He was being selfish? By spending time with her?

Her brother loved her. Her family loved her. Her sisters had always been her closest and dearest friends.

But no one had ever admitted that they enjoyed spending time with her to an extent that they considered themselves selfish to do so.

The compliment sent warm tingles trickling from her heart to her limbs.

"But you did nothing wrong. *We* did nothing wrong."

He leaned forward, resting his forearms on both knees and staring down at the rug with unfocused eyes.

"Not where my world is concerned, Collette—or your brother's—and whether you like it or not." He turned to meet her gaze. "Your world too."

It was moments like this that the weight of society caught up with her. It reminded Collette of the sinking sensation she had felt when Miss Primm had told her she was terminating her employment.

As much as she'd like to convince herself she had choices, in truth, they were far and few between. The small sound that escaped her was supposed to be a protest but ended up sounding almost like a sob.

"Look at me, Collette."

She was incapable of defying him.

"I have kissed you now, on two separate occasions. And if we hadn't been interrupted, it would have been three. To be perfectly frank with you, if—strike that—*when* I have another opportunity, I'll want to do even more. And I think you might as well." He edged closer and that invisible pull had her turning and allowing him to take hold of her hands.

"We must marry, Collette, for both our sakes."

"Not really for your sake." He was a duke! "But you

145

believe it would be for mine."

Two worry lines appeared between his eyes, giving her a glimpse of emotion he normally kept well in check. "Not only for yours. I wish to... I *want* to marry you."

She rubbed her thumb along the back of one of his fingers, thinking that sitting like this felt familiar... And she studied their hands—hers looking almost frail against his, which were not only larger but defined and masculine.

The image. It was... right.

When had this happened?

"But why?" she asked.

Rather than answer, he leaned forward and—

"Oh..."

His kiss, though brief and almost chaste, was worth at least a thousand words.

"Marry me, Collette." His words came out as a demand, a question, and a plea all at once and somehow broke through the turmoil she felt from the unexpected gesture.

He wouldn't ask if he thought she would fail as miserably as she thought she would—if he truly believed her to be vulgar and unladylike—would he?

Was it possible that *this*, that *he*, in fact, was her best choice?

By marrying him, she would no longer face a future where she depended on her brother for the rest of her life, nor would she have to consider marrying some other gentleman, one she had no feelings for.

She wouldn't have to consider taking positions hundreds of miles distant from the people she loved most in the world. She could have children of her own. Children who would have Addison for a father.

And most importantly of all, she could spend her life

getting to know Addison better.

His eyes searched hers, his expression grim even as he awaited her answer. "Please."

Yes.

It was she who leaned forward this time, lifting her mouth in invitation. "Mhmm," she uttered, closing her eyes.

"Yes?" He was close, the warmth of his breath dancing in the air near her lips. But he was not kissing her.

"Yes," she clarified. "But you are supposed to kiss me now." She kept her eyes closed and didn't sigh in relief until he closed the distance between them.

Collette thrilled when he loosened his grip on her hands to settle his arms around her back. The kiss was not brief, nor was it going to be chaste.

~

ADDISON HAD EXPECTED MORE of an argument from her. He'd expected her to insist it wasn't necessary and to ask him for time to decide—a week, at the very least.

He certainly had not expected the rush of triumph that shot through him at her acceptance.

"Yes," he echoed against her lips, which parted easily, inviting him to deepen this kiss. She liked intimacy; she'd wanted this—perhaps as much as he did.

Her lips tasted even sweeter this morning than they had yesterday, and her body molded against his as though she had been made for him.

A soft moan vibrated through her as she wound her arms around his neck. Perhaps they were both relieved to have this matter settled between them—a tired relief that one experienced upon surrendering to fate.

Even though he didn't believe in fate.

She surprised him in her eagerness, her hands in his hair, tugging him closer and demanding that he deepen this connection. She was not, it seemed, inclined to deny her own desires. Anticipation flickered that she might pleasantly surprise him again and again in the years to come.

One hand supporting her, his other was free to explore her shape—down her arm, around her front. He heeded the sounds of her breathing, wanting to understand what she liked, wanting to meet her needs—her desires.

His tongue tangled with hers and when he bit down just hard enough to trap it, she gasped.

He drew back, watching her expression. "You aren't afraid?"

She blinked, her eyes taking a moment to focus. "Should I be?"

He'd made a myriad of mistakes with her, done nothing to earn her trust, and yet, it seemed, she would give it freely.

"No." His urge to protect her swelled. So much so, that he barely noticed the annoying unease pricking at the back of his neck. Because the two of them would meet with obstacles. All marriages did.

Now, however, was not the time to discuss his mother.

"Just kiss me and I won't be afraid of anything." She licked her lips and her pupils dilated, making her eyes appear darker than usual.

Lusty thoughts had him dipping his mouth to the curve of her neck. "I can do that." He covered her breast with his palm, dipping his fingers inside the gap at the top of her bodice. His lips located her pulse, fluttering rapidly as he tugged downward.

"I like this kissing, Addison."

"Very good," he approved. "Collette."

Collette. He rolled her name around his mind. It would seem she'd captured him with nary a shot fired.

"Beautiful." Her breasts were perfectly plump, tilted up, the tips turgid and rosy. A pink flush crept across her skin. "So if you are afraid, shall I kiss you here?" He grazed his lips along tender skin. "What about here?" He dragged his tongue in a spiral. "Here?"

He clamped his mouth around one eager peak and her soft moan aroused him beyond decency.

"Please." Her back arched, and her shaking fingers tangled in his hair. Squirming against him, she seemed frantic, but she wasn't pushing him away, she was pulling him closer.

He sucked her into his mouth, deeper, rolling his tongue over her tight bud. So sweet to taste, so perfect to capture, so utterly feminine. He bit down gently, testing, and her breathing quickened.

"Collette," He growled against her skin.

She was close to release. He sucked sharply, eliciting another moan, and then released her.

"Addison?" she gasped. He loved the sound of his name on her lips. The needy thread in her voice made it even better.

"I want to show you something," he said. But should he?

Her brother was trusting him to be alone with her, but desire reasoned that she'd promised to marry him. She was going to be his wife. And his own need insisted the wedding wouldn't be soon enough. Until then, there was no telling when he would be allowed to be alone with her again.

He wanted to give her something, show her some of what they had to look forward to.

"May I?" He glanced up, needing to read her expression.

From beneath heavy lids, she nodded.

This woman.

The moment he'd stepped into her classroom, he'd been doomed.

Lost.

Felled to his knees.

Being trapped in the stairwell was not the catalyst that had changed the course of his life; meeting this woman had.

Gazes locked, he gathered the material of her skirts and dragged the hem upward. Only when he'd run out of fabric did he allow himself to glance down at the sight he'd revealed.

Slim and shapely legs bent just enough to reveal the tops of silky white stockings. Not silky enough, however, that they were any rival to the tender flesh above them.

He pressed his palm along her inner thigh, drawing slow circles on skin as soft as a butterfly's wings. *"Just kiss me and I won't be afraid of anything."*

"I'll kiss you here." He'd chase all her fears away.

She nodded.

So willing—trusting. Her unquestioning innocence sent his heart racing.

He inhaled, conflicted. She'd said yes. She would taste sweet and delicate but also warm and musky. He dragged his fingertips higher and brushed them over her soft mound of curling hair.

"What are you going to show me?" Her question was barely a shuddery breath.

"Your body is aching, isn't it? I want to take that ache away." He tugged her closer, his fingertips teasing buttery-soft flesh.

His cock was hard and ready, but it was going to have to wait. Another thought, more of a conviction—a knowing—insisted he'd only find his own contentment knowing she was in want of nothing.

He shifted his weight so that she lay partly beneath him along the settee.

"Yes?" He massaged between her folds, his hand slick and wet. Oh, hell. Better than he'd imagined. Tight but also soft and welcoming.

"Yes," she whispered, pressing into him.

He slid in and out, teased by her juices, taunted by her sharp little gasps. If they were anywhere else…

Just as he curled his index finger, stroking deep inside her body, a sound at the door froze him. Collette rotated her hips around his hand and then…

Addison caught her moan in his mouth at the same time he withdrew and covered her quivering mound with his palm.

"Tea will be served momentarily."

Addison met Lady Chaswick's all-too knowing but not completely disapproving glance over the back of the seat. Thank God the settee wasn't facing the door.

"Have the two of you come to a decision?" Her gaze flicked from him to Collette, who was sitting up now and appeared delightfully flushed, her eyes bright and her lips shining.

She twisted around, tucked a strand of hair behind her ear and then smoothed at the wrinkles he'd caused to her skirt.

"We have," she said. "I'm going to give it a go."

ENGAGED

*F*ive days later and Collette had yet to change her mind about marrying Addison, even if he did also happen to be the Duke of Bedwell.

How could she, when her every waking hour was suddenly filled with shopping, social visits, wedding planning and studying? He'd come twice for tea since, looking more handsome with each visit. On one of those afternoons he'd even taken her driving—but there had been no stopping or long talks in a tea house as Polly, of course, had been sent along by Chase to act as chaperone.

On those two days Collette didn't see her fiancé, she unrepentantly relived every second that she'd spent with him, over and over again. She imagined his voice as it had sounded in the stairwell, strained but still proud, the cautious excitement in his eyes when he'd shown her his books, and the sweet sincerity when he'd proposed.

At night, she recalled his hand on her leg, and how he had touched her right before Bethany had interrupted them.

Her face flushing warm at the memory, Collette

dismissed the image and gathered her books onto her bed, crossing her legs beneath her.

All this, and she'd yet to have met his mother and brother, and until Addison was certain his mother had received his letter, they'd decided to hold off on sending any announcements to the Gazette.

Which only served to delay the inevitable, so Collette wasn't about to complain. It meant a few more days of simply being Miss Collette Jones, illegitimate teacher, formerly of Miss Primm's Private Seminary for the Education of Ladies.

Who, if she didn't get to work, would fall behind on the studies with which she'd been tasked.

Miss Robins, the etiquette instructor Chase hired, had departed just before nuncheon, but not before dolling out a few hours' worth of homework, something Collette hadn't expected from a simple course in etiquette.

Collette had glanced through *Debrett's* before, when she'd wanted to look up a particular nobleman's actual title, but never had she considered that she'd be expected to memorize parts of it.

Diana had gotten off easy by marrying Greystone last spring.

Collette sighed and then flipped through the pages before stopping at the page she'd marked. *Brierton, Bedwell, (Duke)*. Since *Debrett's* was stingy when it came to her favorite duke, she closed it and opened the other book which was part of her homework: John Burke's *Dictionary of the Peerage and Baronetage*. Although criticized for some inaccuracies, Burke's book provided a reader with far more detailed information than Debrett's.

Again, she'd placed markers between the most interesting pages.

Bedwell, Duke of, (Addison Holden Brierton) Marquess of St. Alastair, Earl of Samson, Baron Desart, lord-lieutenant and high steward of Bedwellshire, Born February 19th, 1801. Succeeded to the family honors upon the demise of his father in 1822.

Reading through, she noted that all of his ancestors from as far back as 1619 not a single one of them had been born to a man who was lower than an earl. Even if she had been legitimate, she would be a duchess born to the lowest title.

Motto, *honor at all costs.*

The entry listed the locations of both his town residence and country seat, but she knew from speaking with Addison that he held title to several other properties.

A book of great importance amongst the *Ton,* and yet it revealed very little about the actual man—about the caring he felt for his brother and the respect he afforded his mother, about the delightful stories he'd written and had yet to write, and that he had the ability to turn her bones to jelly with a single glance.

Collette deliberately dismissed such thoughts and set her mind to memorizing the list of names and dates of her future relations until, exhausted, she set the book aside and fell backward onto one of her pillows.

She might have been sacked from Miss Primm's, but as far as these studies were concerned, she was determined not to fail.

Laying in gentle repose, Collette closed her eyes and inhaled a deep breath.

She would master these lessons, enjoy the new wardrobe Bethany had ordered for her, and do her best not to collapse under the pressure of all that would be expected of her.

She'd refused to fail Bethany, or Chaswick, or especially Addison.

But most importantly of all, she would not fail herself.

～

ADDISON GLANCED around the vast but sparsely furnished room, taking in the paintings that lined the walls, many of which he'd viewed before but in far less enchanting company.

Almost two weeks had passed since Collette accepted Addison's proposal and he'd yet to have been left alone with her again. Even when he'd taken her driving, Lady Chaswick had insisted a maid ride along.

Every. Single. Time.

Trouble was, before becoming a devoted married man, the baron himself had been something of a rake, which unfortunately, meant he was privy to all the tricks.

Rather than lament their circumstances, however, Addison had taken it upon himself to escort his fiancée to some of his favorite places in London. Always with chaperones in tow—often Lord and Lady Chaswick themselves.

And he was enjoying himself.

Collette had a way of introducing him to new ideas about these old places, and the knowledge she'd shared from her study of Latin had already widened his perspective.

He never knew what to expect, and something about that was particularly freeing.

What wasn't freeing was the sexual tension building from spending time in her company, touching her casually but never more than that, and never being allowed to be alone with her. That vibrating awareness grew more powerful every day—with every glance, with every touch.

He was beginning to think he'd brave locking the two of them inside a coat closet if he could find one.

A glance around had him meeting her brother's watchful eyes. Ah, yes. Chaswick knew all too well the workings of a gentleman's mind. Addison grimaced and shook his head ruefully.

"You smell like sweet cakes this morning," he said softly, for her ears only.

She stopped and leaned in. "You smell like…" She closed her eyes and inhaled just below his chin. They were standing closer to one another than was particularly proper while in public, or anywhere really, but Addison simply waited while she contemplated his scent. "Leather, and… freshly cut wood. And something… something that is uniquely you."

She drew back and met his gaze, blushing, revealing that she, too, was remembering the feel of his intimate touch almost two weeks before.

"Something good, I hope?" Addison cocked a brow.

"Oh, yes. And spicy… perhaps clove." She leaned in to sniff him again. "I'm growing rather fond of it." Damned if the tone of her voice couldn't stir him into a rather inconvenient and potentially embarrassing state.

"Let's keep moving, shall we?" Chaswick spoke from behind them.

"Oh, Chase, look at this one. I think your mother would love having something like this in her suite." Lady Chaswick drew her husband across the room, allowing Addison and Collette a good ten feet of separation as they stepped into a special room of the exhibit.

Ironic that Addison could appreciate and yet resent the man's relentless doggedness at the same time. He adjusted his trousers and forced himself to remember where they were.

"Oh, my." Collette shivered beneath Addison's hand as the two of them arrived at a large painting of a medieval castle. Set on the precipice of a cliff, an angry sea raged against it.

"Do you like this one?" he asked, always intrigued to know her opinion.

If she did, he would buy it for her, perhaps as a wedding gift, even if it was somewhat dark. Not that she ever asked for or expected anything of the sort from him, quite the opposite really. He'd never met a person so apathetic about owning material possessions as his fiancée.

He stared at her while she stared at it.

"I wouldn't describe myself as liking it. It's powerful, though, and depicts an... ill-fated hopelessness."

"You see all of that?"

"The way the sea boils, and the fierce curl of the wave. It's like a monster." The second tremor that ran through her was even stronger.

"So you don't like it?"

"Do you?" She twisted her neck around to meet his gaze responding with a question of her own. "What does it make you feel?"

In the past twelve days since she'd accepted his offer, Addison had learned that his fiancée didn't ask questions without expecting a sincere answer.

He shifted his gaze from her expressive eyes back to the painting and then leaned forward to study it properly.

"Respect for those things that endure," he said, not

filtering his thoughts, something he only found himself doing when he was with her. "It doesn't seem hopeless to me."

She saw a threat in the painting whereas he appreciated the massive stones stacked upon one another, discolored and covered in moss but timeless, practically everlasting.

"Hmm…" she answered softly. "You don't see that the tower is one giant wave away from falling into the sea?" Even her frown had the ability to charm him.

"Not at all."

With a nod, signifying her acceptance of his answer, she turned, and Addison steered them along the corridor to the next painting. Behind them, he could feel her brother watching them.

She leaned closer and the whiff of vanilla he caught had him contemplating options other than closets. Behind a potted plant, perhaps, or…

"I didn't realize you were such an optimist," she said.

"I wouldn't go that far. I'm more of a realist than anything."

The past two weeks of their engagement had consisted of a whirlwind of activity. In between the wedding planning spearheaded by Collette's sister-in law, and her tutoring sessions, Addison had escorted her to the Vauxhall Pleasure Gardens, taken her to examine the curiosities at The Leverian, and today, a special exhibit at the National Gallery in Trafalgar Square.

Tonight Collette and Addison's future in-laws would take in a performance of *Macbeth* as guests in his box at the Theatre-Royal.

Which he'd actually have looked forward to if it was not to be preceded by a formal dinner

Hosted by his mother.

Who had finally arrived in London and Collette would be meeting for the first time.

Addison hated that this thought teased him with a sense of dread.

She was his mother, *blast and damn*. She might prove to be somewhat difficult, but she would accept his decision. Although she had free rein in many things, his choice of wife was not one of them.

"I'm nervous about tonight." Collette's thoughts had apparently jumped to the same place as his. "She's going to hate me."

"It won't be personal." Addison had been honest with Collette regarding his mother's… attitudes. "She'll be like the sea, relentless, punishing and cold, but in the end, nothing she does is going to change a thing. And just like the sea, her storm will pass."

Collette sent him a weak smile.

They'd arrived at a larger painting by now, this one of the same castle, at sunset though. The sea was like glass. "Did you plan this?"

He had not, although the illustration was rather convenient.

"Fate again." His soft chortle mocked himself. When had fate become a part of his vocabulary? "Do you wish I hadn't told you about her letter?"

"No." But her answer was short. "I'll be fine."

The night she'd accepted his proposal, before he'd arranged for the banns to be read at St. George's, Addison had written a letter to his mother and sent it to Brier Manor via special messenger. He hadn't wanted her raising the hopes of any of her guests—or their daughters.

ANNABELLE ANDERS

Nor had he wanted her to read of his betrothal in one of the papers she had delivered from London regularly.

Her response to his missive had come swiftly and left him in no doubt as to her scathing disapproval of the match he'd decided on. He'd hoped for a different response but not really expected anything else.

She'd also given him fair warning as to her pending arrival.

The very next day, he'd relayed the contents of the letter to Collette, over tea and ices at Gunter's.

"She had other candidates in mind for my wife and has whole-heartedly declared our betrothal to be an abomination."

Collette had stared across the table, eyes wide. "Please tell me you are teasing."

"No. I thought you'd want the unvarnished truth."

"I do. I mean, I thought I would. But... you knew she would respond like this! Why didn't you tell me before—"

"Before you pledged your troth to mine?" he'd finished for her.

"Well... yes. I suppose."

"Because I didn't wish to give you more reasons to refuse me." *In that moment, he'd wondered if he shouldn't have insisted on having some privacy for this conversation. That way he'd have been able to distract her from her dismay using tactics that would leave her not giving a damn what his mother thought.*

She'd glared at him and he'd leaned forward, wishing he could soften her mouth with a kiss.

"I am marrying you, not to please my mother, nor to please society, nor even to please your brother," Addison had barely suppressed a frustrated growl. "I'm marrying you because... I want to. And because I believe the two of us will be happy together."

He assumed his response had been what she needed to hear when she'd reached over and squeezed his wrist.

160

The small hand on his arm brought him back to the present. "If she's your mother, she can't be all that terrifying, can she?" Weakness strained Collette's voice.

"She will grow to love you, in time."

He did not add that it might take a decade or two. Adding to her nervousness, at this point, would benefit no one.

～

"I'M GOING TO BE ILL," Collette announced from the backward-facing bench in the carriage as she, Bethany, and Chase drove the short distance to Addison's Mayfair town-house. She rather felt like a woman being carried to the gallows.

"Do we need to pull over?" Bethany asked.

Collette could just make out her sister-in-law's concerned expression in the shadows.

"No. But I wouldn't mind turning around and going home." She knew she sounded like a petulant child, but she'd dreaded this meeting since... even before Addison told her his mother disapproved of their marriage.

She'd known his mother wouldn't approve before she'd accepted him. What duchess in her right mind would want her son marrying someone like Collette?

"Buck up, Cole. It's not as though you're going in there alone." Chase wasn't quite as sympathetic.

"That's right. Bedwell won't stand by and allow her to eat you alive." Bethany actually giggled at this.

He wouldn't. Would he?

"What do I say to her, though? How do I respond when

she insults me?" Because she would. Collette had no doubt of that.

A flash of longing for her own mother swept through her. As a fallen woman, her mother had faced insults nearly every time she'd ventured out. Her mother would have known exactly how to handle the duchess—if only she could have been present tonight. Feeling like she was a child again, the back of Collette's eyes stung.

"Remember what Miss Robins has taught you; take the high road even when you don't feel like it and you will emerge the better person." Miss Robins was the woman hired to instruct her in all matters of social importance. Collette had expected her tutor to be an elderly spinster, stern and unmoving, but instead found herself pleasantly surprised when she'd discovered Miss Robins to be enthusiastic and even inspiring. Collette especially enjoyed that her tutor had a sense of humor—and that she not only taught the rules that must be followed, but explained why they existed in the first place.

And when the reasons were ridiculous, she acknowledged that as well.

"Here we are," Chase announced as the carriage drew to a halt in front of an elegant but not grandiose townhouse. Addison had pointed it out to her on one of their drives, but until tonight, she'd not been invited inside.

It would not have been proper for her to enter her fiancé's residence unchaperoned.

A wave of fear hit her as the carriage door was pulled open, and she drew in a steadying breath while Bethany climbed out in front of her.

"What's the worst that can happen?" Chase met her gaze,

one brow cocked. When she hesitated, he added, "Murder? Bloodshed?"

"No." She couldn't help but giggle at the absurdity of his question. But then she gave the suggestion serious contemplation. "She could always poison my food."

"Have one of the footmen taste each dish before you eat then." Her brother's eyes sparkled enough that she could see he was trying not to laugh.

"But then some poor servant would die."

"I doubt she'll go to those lengths. Too much of a scandal." He held out a hand to assist her to the open door.

Addison awaited her just outside, dressed immaculately and looking so handsome that, for a moment, she forgot all about his mother.

She forgot all about everything except for him.

"I was beginning to think you were going to order your driver to turn around and deliver you back to Byrd House." He clasped her gloved hand in his, the warmth in his gaze wrapping around her. "I'm pleased that wasn't the case."

As the meeting of one's future mother-in-law was a pivotal occasion in any woman's life, Collette and Bethany had gone back and forth determining which gown she ought to wear. And now, glancing down, she was glad they'd decided on the peacock silk.

The cut was delightfully modern, the skirt billowing out from her waist with an asymmetrical lace overlay, tightly fitted bodice, and puffed sleeves that draped on her arm as though tired. She had never worn anything as elaborate.

Addison tucked her hand into the crook of his arm to greet Chase and Bethany.

As a single rider approached from the opposite end of the drive, he dipped his chin. "My brother."

Collette studied the imposing-looking gentleman as he approached their little group. She had been curious about his older brother for almost as long as she'd known Addison, and she couldn't help but search his features for similarities to her fiancé as he dismounted.

"Row, may I present my future bride, Miss Collette Jones. Collette, my brother. Mr. Rowan Stewart."

"Miss Jones, my pleasure." White teeth flashed against the man's bronze skin and when he removed his hat to bow, the waning sunlight reflected off his smooth, equally dark scalp.

"I am pleased to finally meet you." Collette curtseyed, taking note of his fine clothing and a familiar *Bedwellian* tilt to his head. She'd known from what Addison told her that his brother was half Barbadian but aside from his coloring and smoothly shaven head, he seemed more English than anything else.

As Addison introduced the man to Chase and Bethany, Collette appreciated the obvious affection he had for his younger brother. It was the first time she'd seen her fiancé in the company of anyone other than casual acquaintances or her own family.

And if his brother was such a kind gentleman, how horrible could Addison's mother be?

"Mother's waiting in the drawing room." Addison gestured toward the door where a somber butler stood holding it wide.

Mr. Stewart grimaced at the announcement and sent her a pitying glance. "I would wish you luck," he surprised her by saying, "if I thought it would help."

"Well then," she exhaled, willing her feet to walk up the

steps to the door. "In case I don't come out alive, it was a pleasure meeting you."

"You can do this," Bethany whispered loudly from behind her. At least if Collette was to be dropped from the gallows, she wouldn't have to endure it alone.

The ceiling in the foyer was three stories high, with a wide staircase on the right, and elaborate molding framing every angle. Paintings hung on the ivory-colored walls, and a few busts were placed on pedestals. When one noticed the flowers in out of the way niches, and vases, it was, all in all, decidedly overwhelming.

Was the effect intentional?

A giant crystal chandelier hung over head, and the flooring was a cool white marble threaded with grays and silvers.

It was pristine, perfect, cold, and she was helpless at suppressing the shiver that ran through her when she handed her coat over to the unsmiling butler.

"This way, Collette." Addison led her to a set of large double doors on the left, held open by two uniformed footmen.

At the very least, she expected to see the woman seated on one of the long settees, but the room appeared empty. That was, until she caught sight of the woman standing at the window, presenting her back to her guests.

"Mother." Addison's voice echoed off the marble.

"Bedwell." The woman's cultured voice could have cut the glass she was staring through.

"Allow me to present my fiancée." He spoke with his normal conviction and Collette hoped she would sound half as confident.

"But you are not betrothed." The woman turned around, holding herself regally.

The duchess's hair was mostly gold but had tiny threads of silver and had been pinned ornately atop her head. The gown she wore, simple and timeless, made Collette feel gauche and unsophisticated. His mother was one of the most beautiful women she'd ever seen.

The woman's gaze flicked to Chase and Bethany. "Nothing personal, Chaswick. Although I must admit, your father had the right idea, keeping them out of the public eye."

Chase's eyes narrowed but Bethany cleared her throat beside him.

"Good evening, Your Grace. Looking lovely as usual." Mr. Stewart was the last to slip inside, a second undercurrent entering with him despite his compliment.

And although the duchess appeared almost serene, she was not at all successful at hiding her feelings for Addison's brother. Even from across the room, it was all too apparent to anyone with eyes, that she hated him.

Undaunted, Mr. Stewart moved across to a large sideboard to pour himself a drink from one of the amber-filled crystal decanters.

"Of course, by all means, avail yourself to my liquor, Rowan." Addison's mother had yet to even acknowledge Collette's presence, and surprisingly, rather than feel embarrassed for herself, Collette felt embarrassed for the duchess.

Her own mother, a kept woman who'd been spurned by all of society, would never treat guests so rudely.

Collette stepped away from Addison. "I am Miss Collette

Jones." She would not cower. She'd cowered for Mrs. Metcalf and that had gotten her nowhere.

The duchess's eyes finally landed on her. They were the same color as Addison's but might as well have been chips of ice.

"Miss Jones," she deigned to respond, but before Collette could drop into her practiced curtsey, the woman turned her attention to Addison. "I took the liberty of inviting a few special guests. Lord and Lady Huntly and their daughter. You remember Lady Isabella, don't you? Such a beauty —the perfect English Rose, as they say."

So this was to be the duchess's first gambit... The woman had only agreed to this dinner at Addison's request. It was to have been a small "family" affair. By not abiding by her son's wishes, she'd revealed something about herself.

She lacked the honor her son had in spades.

Collette flicked her glance between the two. By now she recognized the subtle ticking in his jaw and the manner in which he twisted his ducal ring on his finger. Aside from those two giveaways, he hid his annoyance well.

More guests appeared at the door, an elderly couple with a petite lady behind them. With a start, Collette realized that she was already acquainted with the duchess's "special guests."

She and Diana had met Lady Isabella last spring. The young woman looked to be barely ten and seven and she was, indeed, a beauty.

She was also the same woman the Marquess of Greystone had passed over in favor of marrying a woman who was not at all respectable or suitable, but happened to be the woman he loved.

Collette's sister.

And Collette would feel sorry for the girl if it wasn't *her* fiancé that Lord Huntly had set his sights on now.

Addison drew Collette closer at the same time the duchess clasped her hand around his other arm. "You'll allow me to steal him away for a moment, won't you, dear? To greet our guests?" Her smile wouldn't have seemed anything but genuine but for the venom in her eyes.

Addison released her with a reluctant grimace.

Take the high road. Her tutor's advice echoed in her thoughts. The high road did not involve playing tug of war with one's fiancé.

Nodding, she dropped her hand and stepped back.

～

ADDISON KNEW his mother's games all too well; he'd watched her play them on numerous occasions. In the past, they'd been mostly harmless.

It had been a mistake for him to think they would be harmless tonight.

Rowan was used to it. His brother had refused to allow the duchess to estrange him from Addison and Fiona and had long since learned how to fight his own battles.

But Collette, despite her intrepid spirit, was out of her depths.

As he shook Lord Huntly's hand, and then bowed to the man's wife and daughter, Addison refused to be distracted from the woman he was intent upon celebrating that night.

"I was unaware that you were joining us this evening," he announced, turning so as to include all of his guests in their conversation. "However, my fiancée and I are happy to share our celebration with others, aren't we, Collette?"

Addison's mother gasped beside him, and he couldn't help but be aware of Lord Huntly's displeasure.

Addison ignored them both in favor of admiring the woman he intended to marry.

Rather than cower in the face of his mother's nastiness, she looked proud... and radiant.

And in that moment, he had no doubt that she would succeed wholeheartedly at anything she set her mind to.

His sweet girl dipped her chin almost haughtily, squared her shoulders, and moved toward him, looking graceful, and by God, every inch the duchess she would soon become.

"What a wonderful surprise it is to see you again, my lady." Her lips tilted up just enough to make her greeting welcoming.

A duchess, indeed.

Etiquette demanded that he present Collette to the earl and countess, but she was already acquainted with their daughter. After they'd wed, even earls and marquesses would be presented to her. But first they had his mother to navigate.

He kept one hand on the small of Collette's back, determined not to fall into any of the other traps that would have been laid out for the evening.

He loved his mother, he always would, but he refused to allow her to treat his future duchess with anything but respect.

When Collette had refused his initial proposal, at the school, all those weeks ago, this was precisely the sort of thing she had dreaded. And yet tonight she had knowingly entered the lion's den.

For him?

For both of them?

But it was also for her. And seeing her like this, he determined to be at least half as brave. His challenge, he already knew, would be supporting his fiancée without having to dishonor his mother.

"And my future sister- and brother-in-law." Addison gestured toward Lord and Lady Chaswick.

"We are already acquainted with the baron and baroness." Lady Huntly's tone was clipped. "But we had always understood him to be his father's only child."

Chaswick's gaze hardened, and, in that moment, Addison gratefully realized that he and Collette did not face the evening without reinforcements.

"I am my father's only son," Chaswick provided. "But I have three sisters."

Addison knew Collette enough to realize that watching her brother defend her would not be easy. "And for that," he inserted, "I, for one, am exceedingly glad."

"Dinner is served, Your Grace."

Beneath his hand, Addison felt Collette's exhale of relief at the interruption. More than once, he'd wondered if the dinner was a mistake, he'd wondered even, if he should have simply married Collette in a private ceremony, by special license, and later presented his new bride to his mother as a *fait accompli*.

But he didn't want her to think he was ashamed of her in any way, nor did he want society to think the same.

"I am honored to escort your fiancée into dinner." Rowan stepped away from the wall where he'd been watching the drama unfold. "And might I add, bravo. First points of the evening to the bridegroom. I'm quite looking forward to more of the same."

His brother, perhaps even better than Addison, understood his mother's games. They were usually played at Rowan's expense.

Addison relinquished Collette regretfully, but he was certain she would be safe with Row. Perhaps Rowan would provide her with a few suggestions for dealing with the duchess.

"At least you haven't forgotten all of your manners." His mother appeared at his side to take hold of his arm. The others paired up according to rank to follow them through to the dining room. Collette and Rowan, of course, would be last.

"Why would you imagine I had forgotten any?" Addison refused to allow her to goad him.

"She's positively vulgar in comparison to Lady Isabella. Surely you must see that. Honestly, Addison, I cannot imagine what you've been thinking. Why can't you simply take her as a mistress? She's practically been raised for that. Even with the baron's obvious stubbornness, surely you and that woman can come to some other—er—private arrangement."

"Don't push me, Mother." But she had already gone too far. Should he bring the evening to an inauspicious ending in light of her behavior?

Collette was smiling now at something Rowan was saying.

He'd wait.

So long as she was holding up, he would as well.

"Lady Isabella is perfect for you, Bedwell. You've known

for some time that she's at the top of my list. Greystone was a fool to allow her to get away last spring."

A footman pulled out the chair at the foot of the table for his mother, and Addison waited at the opposite end until all the ladies were seated before taking his own.

Collette sent him a reassuring glance from a few settings away, still looking confident. Ironic, really. He ought to be the one reassuring her.

Rowan sat beside her, and just across from them, Lady Isabella.

Lady Isabella's father sat at his right, of course, as the highest-ranking male guest. What had his mother expected? That he would discuss marriage contracts with the man?

It ought to have been Chaswick seated there—his future brother-in-law.

Lifting the wine glass to his lips, Addison clenched his jaw. He would not accept responsibility for keeping Lord Huntly happy. His mother had led the earl to believe Addison wished to court their daughter, and so he would leave it to her to make the necessary apologies.

As the first delicacy of the evening was served, Addison sat back quietly, allowing conversation to proceed without him. He was, in fact, content to enjoy the various wines he'd ordered while observing Collette charm those seated around her—surprisingly, even Lady Isabella and the girl's mother.

As though sensing she'd gone too far, his own mother held her tongue through the first few courses. But Addison would not drop his guard. He had no doubt it was only a retreat, not a full-out surrender.

He gestured for the footman to fill his glass.

In the end, the duchess wasn't going to win. Addison

was going to marry Collette and if his mother couldn't accept that gracefully, he'd send her away to where her disapproval wouldn't matter.

"Have you had a chance to view the latest exhibit at the National Gallery yet?" Lady Chaswick brought up their outing earlier that day. "The display is a rather magnificent one."

"Lady Isabella is an excellent painter, is she not, my lord?" Addison's mother suddenly came to life.

"Indeed. We have a room set aside in Battleford Park, where we have them displayed." Lady Huntly enthused. "You must visit, Your Grace, in order to truly appreciate the extent of her talents."

"Perhaps sometime after the wedding." Addison leaned back, unwilling to discuss Lady Isabella and her many talents. Not that she wasn't a pleasant young lady, but he'd leave the regaling of her talents for some other bachelor.

"Several months after," Addison added, feeling goaded. "As I'm considering a tour of the Continent for our wedding journey. How would you feel about that, Collette?"

It was beyond rude of him to dismiss the countess's invitation so casually, and yet some devil prodded him, nonetheless.

Even Collette looked nonplussed by his brutish behavior. Of course, she would be taken aback by it; she'd been tutored daily on proper behavior in the few weeks since they'd become engaged,

She flicked a glance to her sister-in-law, and then back to him before answering, "I think that would be wonderful."

"Enough, Addison," his mother hissed.

"You'll be finished with your project by the time we return, eh, Row?" He ignored his mother. "And if you decide to sell, perhaps my duchess would prefer that we take up residence in a more modern home."

"If we can keep the vandals away. I'm going to have to hire a few men to guard the site, it seems, if I'm to avoid further delays."

Chaswick leaned forward in his chair. "The new manor on Park Street? I, for one, was glad to see Odwick's torn down. It had become quite the eyesore. What exactly are your plans?"

Everyone present seemed a little relieved to listen to Rowan explain the design, the advantages of that piece of property, and the plans he had to invigorate the gardens.

"And this is for yourself?" Lady Chaswick asked.

"I haven't yet decided." Rowan met Addison's gaze. "You are welcome to give Miss Jones a tour."

Addison rubbed his chin. Living somewhere separate from his mother was a rather appealing idea.

"But there is no need," his mother snapped. "As Bedwell, it's only fitting that you reside in your ancestral home."

"Brier House is barely a hundred years old," he pointed out. "Not exactly ancestral."

"What about Fiona?" His mother obviously did not appreciate the direction of this conversation. Not if she was willing to bring Fi into it.

"She could stay at either."

"You are not moving out of Brier House, and you are not marrying that woman." Such an outburst from his mother, from *a duchess*, invoked a wave of discomfort not easily dismissed.

Chaswick moved to stand but his wife stayed him with a wince. Rowan shook his head and it appeared Lady Huntly and her daughter might simultaneously burst into tears.

Even Lord Huntly shifted in his seat.

But it was the expression on Collette's face that caused Addison's heart to drop.

"Excuse me." She struggled to push her chair back until one of the footmen stepped forward to assist her.

"Most unfortunate, Bedwell. We'll be taking my sister home now." Chaswick was assisting his wife up as well and turned his glare on Addison's mother. "I wish I could say it's been a pleasure, Your Grace. However, in the light of your reception, I'll refrain."

"Let's do it again sometime." Rowan was leaning back in his chair, looking far more entertained than was necessary, and for a fleeting second, but not for the first time, Addison wished it was he who had been born out of wedlock.

"We're done here." Addison rose, tossing his napkin on his chair. He'd allowed this to go too far. "Lord Huntly, Lady Huntly. My apologies, Chaswick, my lady."

He didn't bother with any other niceties as he bolted from the room, anxious to catch up to Collette who'd already managed to flee.

He needed to get to her. He'd purchase that special license and they could be married by this time tomorrow.

Damn his mother to hell.

He'd grown rather fond of the idea of marrying Collette. More than fond, actually. His heart squeezed at the possibility that Collette might change her mind.

"Miss Jones wished to relay to her family that she will meet them at home." Addison's butler was all disapproval as he imparted Collette's message. Sensing excitement, Zeus and Hera appeared in the entry as well.

"Tell Lord Chaswick I'll ensure her safe return." And

without bothering to wait for an answer, Addison flew out the door.

He was so intent on catching up with her, he didn't bother rebuking the dogs when they raced along the walk beside him.

TOO HIGH OF EXPECTATIONS

*C*ollette's hand trembled as she brushed a tear away. She'd known she would not be welcomed by his mother. She'd known joining his family was going to be an uphill climb. But not in a thousand years would she have believed the duchess could be so impossibly rude.

The Duchess of Bedwell hated her. The woman had made assumptions as to Collette's character knowing only the circumstances of her birth. Collette had suspected this would be the case. She'd not for a second believed his mother would accept her, let alone welcome her.

She was all the more annoyed with herself for hoping for anything different.

Head down, Collette marched along the walk, hating that she'd lost control to the extent that she'd stormed out of Addison's home in a fit of temper—hating that the duchess had been able to hurt her.

Breaking down like this was most unbecoming of a lady. Sometime during dinner, it seemed, she'd missed the turn that would keep her on the high road.

A sound came out of her, part sob, part laugh, part horror.

Her manners had never been the problem. There was no level of proper behavior that could ever overcome the way his mother viewed her.

Such animosity was only so great, Collette knew, because the woman wanted the best for her son.

It was Collette, not his mother, who had placed him in this predicament. All because she wanted him! Of course, she wanted him. She might possibly even love him.

No "might possibly" about it.

She loved him.

And she was hurting him in the process.

If she and Addison were to marry, a deep chasm would grow between him and his mother. And what of his sister?

He'd never told Collette he loved her. He liked kissing her. He enjoyed her company. But even if he did love her, how long before he resented her for tearing apart his family?

And then there was her own family to consider. Chase and Bethany had gone out of their way, risked their place in society in order to open up opportunities for her and Diana and Sarah.

The duchess would not take a marriage between Collette and Addison laying down. No doubt, she would use every chance she could to disparage her new daughter-in-law. And in doing so, cause trouble for everyone Collette loved.

Ah, yes, she'd learned more from Miss Robin than she'd thought.

And she'd been fooling herself, playing along with this charade of an engagement.

"Collette!" Addison called from behind her.

She wanted nothing more than to run into his arms, but new doubts... old one's really, revived by his mother, held her back.

"You shouldn't follow me," she shouted over her shoulder. But neither should she be walking alone, with darkness setting in quickly. A couple strolling along the opposite side of the street stared at her curiously.

She didn't want to care, and yet she did. *Curses!*

"Collette." Of course, he easily caught up with her, not even out of breath.

Two dogs trotted along at his heels. Zeus, and Hera, she had no doubt.

A sideways glance confirmed that he was not at all happy. She could tell by the small ticking along his jaw.

"Are you angry with me?" she asked.

He deserved to be, just as she deserved to be angry with him. But Collette wouldn't be so easily fooled into fighting with him over something his mother had done.

"I'm angry with myself," he growled as he slowed his steps to match hers. "I never should have put you, nor your family, in that position." He ran a hand through his hair in obvious frustration. "I mistakenly assumed my mother would defer to my wishes. God, she was horrible. I should have known..."

"You are not responsible for her actions." Collette exhaled. "But tonight, it's shown me more than ever that you and I—"

"Don't say it." He tensed beside her, noticing that the other couple on the street was staring outright by now. "This way. I want to show you the house Rowan's building. We can talk without interruption there."

Addison glanced around and then sighed at the two dogs

who were staring up at him panting, tails wagging back and forth in adoration.

"What are you two doing here?" He lowered himself to rub the larger dog's back.

"Zeus and Hera?" Collette dropped down beside him, welcoming any distraction from the turmoil that had been dinner.

On her haunches, Collette folded her hands in front of her and watched him. Addison was even more adorable with his dogs.

This wasn't at all fair.

"Hello, sweethearts." She smiled at the smaller, Hera. "Aren't you beautiful?"

Addison slid his glance her way. "I have a thing for beautiful women."

Not fair at all.

"Go on home, Zeus, Hera." He rubbed each of their heads. "I need to talk with Collette. Go on." He rose and gestured back toward the house. "Home." The dogs obeyed but not without a few sorrowful glances back at him.

"I think I'm in love." She laughed. "They followed you."

"And I followed you." But his stare could hardly have been more somber.

Addison assisted her to her feet, and they resumed walking. With a destination in mind, now, he all but dragged her past the almost identical facades of homes that belonged to London's elite.

This was one of the most exclusive neighborhoods in all the world, and yet, she—an illegitimate woman, with a mother some accused of being a whore—also considered Mayfair her home. The peace of the darkening sky calmed her.

She belonged and yet she didn't. She was good enough, and yet she wasn't.

"This isn't going to work, Addison. Your mother is right."

"She's wrong," he answered.

"But I can't—"

"You can," he growled. How had she not realized how stubborn he could be?

The paved walks felt hard beneath her slippered feet as the two of them strode along in silence. Just when she was ready to draw him to a halt, they turned a corner and a partially built manor, all but hidden by scaffolding, appeared.

Mr. Stewart's house. It must be.

Despite it only being partially completed, the structure had more personality than she had expected. Featuring two turrets and several niches, one might think it fussy or overly ornate, but it was neither of those things.

"It's incredible," she said, suddenly curious as he opened a tall iron gate and waved her to enter before him. The garden, as far as she could see, had obviously been neglected for years but was not without potential.

"We should be able to enter in the back. Rowan will have kept some flints there." Addison led her along a flagstone path but was shaking his head. "What was I thinking, bringing you here at nightfall?"

"How could you have known? It isn't as though either of us planned this." In fact, they ought to be having dessert about now. And then readying to leave for the theater.

Addison flicked her a wry smile before squeezing her hand and slipping the two of them through an arched opening. Long shadows made it nearly impossible to see where they were walking.

"*Collette.*" They'd hardly stepped inside before Addison turned and backed her against the cool wall. His mouth claimed hers almost violently, but Collette welcomed the sudden onslaught.

The sky could have fallen, the world could have opened up and swallowed them—and none of it would have mattered.

He broke the kiss just as abruptly and buried his face against her neck. "I'm sorry."

This large, proud, and powerful man seeking refuge in her arms evoked an overwhelming desire to comfort. It was similar to how she'd felt the day she'd helped him in Miss Primm's stairwell weeks ago.

But she had not loved him then. Not quite two months and yet it felt like a lifetime had passed.

His lips found hers again, and as he explored her taste, she slid her hands up his chest and around his neck.

Needing closer—*needing more*--she raised one leg, tightening it around his thighs. She could fight her own desperation but... she didn't want to.

Addison lifted her off the ground and she instinctively wrapped both legs around his waist.

She'd been allowed to see him on numerous occasions since accepting his proposal, but always with a companion or in public. Unable to be alone together, this pull had become nearly unbearable. And now she had him to herself. This was what she'd wanted. This was what she'd needed.

The freedom to surrender—to relinquish the restraints imposed by nearly everyone around them.

She wanted more than his hands touching her. She wanted to be filled with him, joined to him.

"I want you," he murmured against her mouth.

"Yes." More than air itself. Collette tightened her arms and wiggled her hips in an attempt to be closer. She wanted him.

Closer.

Inside.

"Addison." She couldn't marry him, could she? But she wanted him, she needed him.

She loved him.

He moved them away from the wall, carrying her across the heavily shadowed room to lower her onto a cot. She hadn't noticed it before.

She looked at him in surprise and he shrugged.

"My brother is very dedicated."

But Collette didn't require any explanations. She lifted her mouth to his again. All she knew was Addison. Breathing the same air—touching her—kissing her.

Loving her.

The last glimmer of dusk stole through the door and in mere minutes, they'd be in total darkness. But for now, she could still make out the expression on his face—the light shining in the back of his eyes.

This was love. It could be nothing but love. How could she not surrender to love?

"*Collette,*" he breathed.

She sunk into the thin mattress and held out her arms to welcome him.

Over her—on her. *In her.*

Her fingertips brushed the corner of his lips and he smiled.

Oh, but his smile was so very precious.

He is precious.

"I'm sorry about your mother," she whispered.

Was it possible his mother had hurt her own son more than she'd hurt the woman she'd intended to frighten off? Because a person could hurt you so much more when you loved them. And of course, Addison loved his mother. She was the woman who'd given birth to and raised him.

But it was also obvious that she was very, very bitter. In that instant, Collette knew that his mother hated that his father had loved another woman first. Had the previous duke loved his wife at all?

Addison shook his head. "I don't want to talk about my mother right now."

"We'll talk about whatever you want."

Addison hovered over her, protecting her from his weight with his arms.

He cocked one brow wickedly. "You wish to talk?"

Not really. She wanted him. She wanted all of him. But...

"I love you."

She hadn't meant to confess her feelings so abruptly, but her heart overflowed. She was powerless to keep them inside.

"I do. I just do," she admitted again.

He stilled and when he didn't answer right away, she wished she could see his face better.

"You, *my love*." His voice caught. "You are the sunshine on my soul. All my life, there has been this shadow... but since the day we met, I've felt your light."

"I was an annoying teacher." She remembered the moment he'd stepped into her classroom, all top lofty and irritated.

"Exactly what I needed—what I still need—so infuriatingly optimistic; eager to make a difference. You never once pretend to be anyone but who you are. And you... you *saw me.*"

He lowered his forehead to hers, his head heavy even though he braced most of his weight above her, his elbows bracketing the sides of her face. "I'm not expressing myself very well."

She was his sunshine? How was it possible for words to squeeze her heart?

"Oh, but you are." Collette widened her knees and was rewarded with the feel of his weight and his manhood, turgid, teasing the ache blossoming between her thighs.

When had she known she loved him? Had she begun to fall when they'd been trapped together in that ridiculous stairwell?

Was it fate that had brought them together? Because the two of them would otherwise never have known one another.

They belonged to different worlds.

Impossibly different worlds.

"Touch me?" she all but choked on an assault of emotions—emotions ranging from incredulous need to raw desperation.

She loved him.

I love him!

"My sunshine. My light." He deftly lowered her bodice.

The cool breeze that hit her skin ought to have cooled the shooting heat in her veins. Instead her temperature spiked.

Latching onto her breast, he stoked a fire with his

tongue and with a tugging sensation. Sharp teeth grazed tender flesh, making her pant. "Please," she begged.

If this was all she could take from him, she was going to take everything. She fumbled at the opening of his trousers.

Was she like her mother after all? Had her mother become her father's mistress, not because it had been her only choice, but because it had been the *best* choice? Had her mother laid claim to the best of both worlds by taking the only parts of him that he could offer?

Because Addison was making her feel oh, so very, *very* good.

She ought to be embarrassed by the wetness he found between her legs. Any proper lady should feel embarrassed.

"You're so damned soft and wet. Beautiful for me, love." Wicked fingers located her opening and he slid one inside, entering her easily. And then another.

She tugged at the waist of his trousers, impatient for more because apparently, her lessons in propriety hadn't gone far enough.

"For you," she gasped.

He was everything to her and when she wrapped her hand around his thick, throbbing manhood, she wanted it inside of her. It was hot and silky but also rigid.

"Dear God." She had never known. How had she never known?

Proper ladies be damned. She gave a gentle squeeze and rubbed her thumb over the tip where she found a bead of liquid. His seed. She drew lazy circles and squeezed again.

"Holy hell, Collette," Addison whispered against her skin. "You're perfect. Always."

"And yours," Collette gasped, aching, opening. "I'm yours."

"And I'm yours." He covered her hand with his and helped glide the silken shaft along her seam. With each stroke, he spread her juices along his length. This was right. This was what they'd been created for.

"Yes," She lifted her hips, hungry for more. She'd heard there would be tearing and braced herself for the promised pain of losing her maiden head.

She didn't care. All she could think was, *Fill me. Take me.* Both of them thrust at the same time and… "Oh!" A ripping feeling deep inside.

He felt it too and froze. "God, Collette. I hurt you."

"No." Her need was sharper than any pain. "Don't stop. Don't stop." *I love you.*

He withdrew and then edged inside again. "I love you, Collette."

"Right there." *I love you.* He came into her deeper.

"All of you."

"Mine." Collette exhaled. He was big, bigger than she had imagined it could be, but her inner flesh stretched and cradled him. They were no longer separate halves.

Making love with Addison was more than a joining, it was a transformation.

"Love you," he chanted, rocking into her. She lifted her hips and as he moved in and out, they fell into perfect rhythm.

"Love you," she echoed, clutching him with her legs, her arms… her soul.

If she let go, surely, she would shoot into the sky, out of her body, never knowing the limitations of the physical world again.

On the tails of that very fanciful thought, Collette felt Addison stiffen and then plunge deeper, releasing a warmth that could only be his seed, and the most exquisite pleasure struck her like lightning.

The universe tipped and then swirled into a vortex, and rather than join the stars, she became one of them.

She shuddered, and cried out, the roaring in her ears sounding like thunder.

"What the hell?" Addison lifted his head.

The roaring was not in her ears. It was coming from overhead. And there were other earthly, very real crashing sounds mixed with it.

Something was horribly, horribly wrong. At the same time snapping wood shook the room, Addison rolled both of them onto the floor and under the frame of the metal cot.

Her head slammed against the cold hard floor, and she burrowed herself against Addison's body as dust and stones and wood that surely must be the entire house came crashing down.

The physical world, it seemed, would take its revenge for the two of them daring to step outside of it.

Crumbling, raining, a few more snaps and then...

Silence.

TRAPPED AGAIN

*S*he was safe.

Addison had not even begun to recover from what had been the most exquisite experience of his life when he'd heard the first piece of wood splinter and give way.

"Collette, sweetheart, are you hurt?"

"I don't think so. Mostly," she answered, her voice a little shaky. "I always wondered what it would be like, but I never expected it to be earth shattering."

Addison chuckled, relieved, and then inhaled. The scent of dust and debris nearly overpowered the scent of her, and of their lovemaking. But not quite.

She had been a revelation. But he couldn't dwell on that now. He needed to assess their situation.

And he very much intended to do just that—if only he could bring himself to move. Or open his eyes. Or do anything.

But they were trapped beneath this cot—trapped in this

very small space. His chest was beginning to tighten as terror slithered up his spine.

"Collette." He hated the fear in his voice as he fought this brewing panic.

"What kind of man are you? A weakling? A sniveling girl?"

It was his father's voice.

The old duke loomed over him, angry from catching him running to Rowan's room, upset from a nightmare.

"I dream about the bog," he explained and then watched as disgust twisted his father's expression.

"Not that again. I'll teach you to be a man, by God."

He felt himself being lifted over the window seat used for storage in his father's study. Sensing his fate, knowing the world was about to swallow him whole, Addison began fighting, kicking, and screaming.

And begging.

"Whip me instead, Father." He cried. "Please, I'll never do it again. I promise."

"Not the box! You know he hates it." Their father pushed Rowan back. "Punish me instead."

Not even the favored son could cut through their father's stubbornness once his temper took over.

"You'll get over this foolishness one way or another." His father pushed him down mercilessly, tucking Addison inside.

The sounds of the lid closing, and then the lock—

"Addison." Collette's voice cut through his memory. "Addison. I'm here."

He inhaled.

Collette. Vanilla. Her skin. Her taste.

Tender hands soothed his shoulders, his arms. "I'm here."

He nodded. And then inhaled her scent again. He needed to get her to safety in case the entire structure gave out.

God help him, he needed to gauge their situation before he lost control of his fear completely.

Because if their situation was as dire as he thought it was, his heart would explode before anyone even discovered they were trapped here.

But it wasn't his life that mattered. It was Collette's.

In fact, Collette was all that mattered. He nodded again, inhaled, and forced his eyes open.

Black. Black everywhere.

"Are you all right?" He pressed his mouth to the top of her head.

Sweet and warm. He inhaled again, filling his senses with... *her.*

When she didn't answer right away, he moved his hands over her shoulder. "Collette?"

"My foot..." A tremor shook her voice. Addison froze. She'd try to hide her fear from him—his brave Collette. She'd been brave from the moment he met her. "Something's caught it."

"Does it hurt?"

"A little. More now. But..." She gasped. "It's trapped."

His heart skipped a beat. The possibility that her foot was crushed only increased his urgency to get the two of them out from beneath this damn house. She would need a physician, and quickly.

If he failed... He thrust away the wave of fear and hopelessness that wouldn't help anything and steeled himself.

Reaching down to free her from his position was impossible. Only a few inches of empty space surrounded them.

Addison swallowed hard. The cot had saved them from being crushed outright. It was as though they'd been entombed—buried alive.

Before panic could crush him again, he rejected such thoughts.

He'd make damn sure they didn't die here together.

An opening. There must be gaps in the debris. He'd locate one and then he'd ensure it had sufficient supports for them to pass under.

"Can you move your foot at all?"

"Oh!" She gasped. "I can, but... Addison, it hurts." The pain in her voice tore at him.

"Don't move it then, love. I'll free you. I'm going to get us out of here." All he wanted to do was hold her, reassure her, and make all her pain go away. First, though, he needed to save her. "Trust me?"

"Yes."

Sliding his arms out from beneath her, he could only make incremental movements but managed to roll so that he faced the outside—or what he thought was outside. Cool air teased his chest.

An opening.

He explored the space with his hands. Fabric. The wool of his jacket on the floor. He didn't even remember taking it off. And wood. Planks, small gaps surrounding most of them.

If he could push the lower half of himself out, then he could turn around enough to free her foot.

"Someone will come, won't they? What if the cot breaks?"

Addison reached behind him and gently squeezed her thigh. "It won't break. I promise."

"I'm sorry." Addison heard—and felt—her attempts to breathe evenly. "You're right. I'm sorry. Of course. I—"

"Love? He cut into her apologies. "I'm going to get us out

of here. I have an idea." Because Rowan's workers would not return until morning and with most of Mayfair's residents vacated until spring, there was no guarantee that anyone had heard the collapse.

This had to have been the work of the vandals Rowan had told him about. There was no way Rowan's construction would ever allow for such a catastrophe.

She found his hand and squeezed. She was scared. His precious, brave girl—hurt and scared. All because he'd brought her here. If only he'd taken her directly to her brother's house instead. Or the park—anywhere but here.

But he couldn't think about that now.

A tremor ran through her small body. Her gown was mostly gathered around her waist.

"You're cold." *Because of him.*

What had he been thinking to place her in danger like this?

"No." Her teeth chattered. And then another tremor. He located his jacket again, shoved it above his head, and turned again to face her.

"Don't worry about me," she protested. "I'm fine. Do what you need to do. I'm fine."

But worrying about her was exactly what was going to get them to safety. She was his sanity. If he worried about himself…

He cradled her face in his hands and then pressed his lips to her forehead. "Do you hurt anywhere else?"

"No. No. Should I scream for help? Would anyone come?"

Addison considered the size of the lot, how far they were from the street, and the thickness of the untended trees and shrubs surrounding them.

But if she thought it would help, and it provided her with a distraction, then he wouldn't discourage her. "It can't hurt." And then he braced himself for her voice to shatter the cool silence around them.

"Help!" Her voice wobbled with her shout. Another shiver. "I don't think I'm much of a screamer."

"Let me help you into this." He opened his jacket, glad that she seemed momentarily distracted from her pain. "Careful, love."

The skin on her arms was cool and damp. And far too delicate for her to be laying in the debris that had worked its way into their small sanctuary.

Addison guided her hand into the arm of his jacket. Never had she seemed so fragile as she did in that moment.

She was his heart, his life, and she was oh, so very vulnerable.

Thank God they'd made it under the cot.

"Let me..." She arched her back so he could slide the jacket under her and working together, the two of them managed to get her covered.

Shielded.

It shouldn't make any difference but knowing she was protected in his jacket provided him with some comfort.

"That's better. It smells like you," she said.

He smiled, calmed by her matter-of-fact observation.

"Still leather and wood?" he asked, wanting to keep holding her but turning again so he could renew his efforts to free her foot.

"I remember it distinctly. From the stairwell. I remembered it even after you left Warstone Crossing."

"You are vanilla and spring—and sometimes mint. My favorite perfume in all the world." He located the opening again and, contorting himself, tucked his knees up and pushed his feet through it.

If he dislodged one of the planks supporting the debris on top of them, he could possibly bring down even more of the structure.

He wasn't sure how much weight the cot could support.

He edged his feet out slowly, taking note of each piece of wood he encountered, how it fit, and which direction it lay, trying to get an idea as to the puzzle of chaos around them.

With most of his lower half out from under the cot, he allowed himself to focus on Collette's predicament again.

Eau du Arousal. Vanilla still, but also muskiness, blended with flowers that blossomed in early spring. He drew in a deep breath. His position placed his head against her thighs, where she was naked with the lower half of her gown drawn up to her waist.

If they hadn't just made love and if he wasn't trapped beneath Rowan's bloody house, by God, he'd—

He kissed her skin, tasting it as he dragged his tongue down her leg.

"Addison?" Her hand landed on his head, and he felt a tug as her fingers threaded in his hair. This wasn't the time or the place, but God help him, he felt himself hardening again.

Which, presently, was not going to help his cause.

"When we get out of here, I'm going to taste every inch of you." He made this promise for both of them.

"I will taste you." The fact that she could surprise him no longer surprised him.

"A thousand times. We have a lifetime, Collette."

He would get them out of here. His resolve could not be greater.

There was a long and happy marriage awaiting them.

He slid his hand over her knee, which was bent, and then down her calves. To her ankle and foot.

He placed a soft kiss on her ankle, and skimmed his fingers over to her other leg, which lay straight, and seemingly locked onto the floor.

Somehow, when he'd rolled them off the cot, he hadn't managed to keep her head high enough and that had left her foot to stick out the bottom of the cot.

He felt around. Two planks were crossed, forming something of an X, making for the perfect trap.

"It's not crushing you?" He had to be sure.

"No. But it's tight."

He exhaled.

Supporting himself with his elbows, he tenderly touched his lips just above her stuck ankle.

"I'm going to go around." He wasn't sure how, but it was the best he could come up with at this point.

"Addison?" Fear and pain and love all managed to sound in her voice.

"I love you, Collette. We're going to get out from under this damned house, and tomorrow, I'm getting a special license. And then, so help me, you and I are going to be married by the bishop if I have to track him to ground myself."

Which he ought to have done all along.

She didn't contradict him.

She didn't say anything.

"Tell me what you're thinking." Addison was crawling out from beneath the cot again, grateful that he was wearing an older pair of boots. The soles were thin, and he could feel the positioning of the planks better that way. "Let's address all of your concerns once and for all."

Now, he supposed, ironically, was as good a time as any.

"Your mother is right," she admitted. "I'm simply not duchess material."

There was a gap to his left and he edged his legs into it. It was larger than he'd expected. He could get them out of here. She would, by God, agree to marry him.

But first he must free her foot.

Very carefully.

"Is it because of how you see yourself?"

"It's because of who I actually am."

He located a small broken board and turned it to stand beneath one of the beams to his right. Hopefully, it would be thick enough to hold if necessary.

A wave of dizziness rolled over him. Without her touch, his fear threatened to crush in around him.

He remembered those moments in the stairwell, when she'd helped him by simply... talking.

"I don't deserve to be a duke any more than you deserve to be a duchess. But it's our fate." There he went again, embracing this notion of destiny—of a predetermined future for both of them.

"But you aren't illegitimate."

"My inheritance is. But for my father's ill-fated decision not to marry Rowan's mother, I'd likely be a soldier, or a cleric." He grunted as he reached to place a support. "But for your father's ill-fated decision to marry your brother's mother, you would have already taken the *Ton* by storm and not given me a second look."

"I'd have given you a second look." Her voice echoed softly from beneath the cot. "And a third."

"Even my father regretted not marrying Rowan's mother." Addison never discussed this with anyone. It was a topic that he and his brother were well adept at avoiding. "Rowan was always stronger than me... My father hated that his legal heir was weak. I was smaller. I was... a disappointment."

～

SHE PICTURED HIM AS A CHILD, again, as she'd imagined—with lighter hair and sweet eyes that would have been innocent and trusting.

"There was a place for storage, a box in my father's study. After he discovered the fear I had, from the bog, he said it was his duty to crush it. And according to my father, that meant making me face it."

Addison paused and then grunted from exertion as he shuffled around. The sound of wood scraping against wood had her holding her breath.

"Be careful. I don't know what I'd do..." She swallowed hard, the thought of losing him was suddenly all too real.

And unbearable.

This man. She'd be half a person without him.

"He locked me in it. You say you're not a screamer. I think I screamed that first time until my voice went raw. He didn't let me out until much later. I either fell asleep from exhaustion or passed out from clawing at the lid. Thereafter, that box was my punishment. For failing at my studies or playing with the wrong children. For doing anything that would tarnish our family's honor. It didn't take long to realize how important it was never to break the rules."

Honor was everything.

No wonder. Dear God. How could a father do that to his own child?

No wonder.

"And your mother didn't stop him?" She brushed away a tear. Had both his parents been monsters?

"She didn't know. Even if she had, I doubt she could have. My father was a very stubborn man." He paused and she heard wood shifting before he continued. "My brother teases me now for always staying within the lines, so to speak. I do believe he was rather thrilled when I told him about you, Collette. Let me know how you are doing."

His story summoned silent tears to stream down her face and she swallowed hard before she could answer. The wood pressing down on her foot felt tighter; she couldn't even twist now. But she didn't want to worry him. He was already doing everything he could.

"Collette?" He seemed to pause what he was doing.

"I'm afraid." But that wasn't going to help. "But I'm well enough."

"You? Afraid?" He was moving again. "You're the one who kept me from weeping like a baby while we were locked in that stairwell... Not sure if I started falling in love with you then, or the moment I came into your classroom and you glared up at me for interrupting your solace."

"You wouldn't have wept."

"Oh, no, I was weeping inside."

Collette remembered. He'd gone pale that day, his breathing had been uneven, but he'd kept most of his emotions in check.

And then she remembered.

"I fell in love with you when you kissed me." She'd tried to deny it, even to herself, but she had.

She really had.

"So it's all about the kissing?" Teasing sounded in his voice. But she wasn't going to limit her confession to how she felt about his kisses. If she was going to die, she was going to tell him all the things she loved about him first.

"I love that you see me differently than anyone else does. How you see me… better than I am."

"I just see you."

"And I love that you make jokes, even when you're pretending to be serious. I love that you're true to yourself, despite the expectations of your position. And I love your stories."

"You haven't read them."

"But I have. Most of them. I went back and bought the entire collection the day after you showed them to me." It had put a sizable dent in her savings but she couldn't help herself.

Silence fell where he'd been working. "You read them?"

"Just the first three so far. And I love them. They paint the most vivid pictures, and your characters come to life on the page. Albert is simply wonderful." His protagonist lived the life of freedom that Addison could not. He'd traveled the world, fought off villains, and met distant people.

"You don't hate them?"

Because they were his, even if they'd been boring and staid, she likely would have read them. And she could never hate anything he created.

But she was able to answer truthfully. "Not at all." She smiled. "And I am not just telling you that because I love you."

Saying the words to him was a freedom in itself.

She wished she could see his face in that moment, and

yet there was a certain intimacy to talking with him in the dark like this.

"All right. I'm going to lever this up and when I do, pull your foot out."

If he moved the wood, more could fall. "What if it sends everything else crashing? Addison, be careful for yourself. Please. If it fell on you—"

"It won't. I won't let it." He sounded so confident that she almost believed him.

She wished he could kiss her first. One last time, just in case.

"I'll kiss you properly when we're out." Oh, but how he knew her.

"All right." She squeezed her eyes together. "I'm ready."

"On three."

"On three," she confirmed. He was going to get them out of this.

"One... two... three!

Collette tried bending her knee, but her ankle caught on the wood and spikes of pain shot up her leg.

And then she felt his hand, turning her foot and wedging it toward her. Dear God, so much pain!

She'd been wrong when she'd told him she wasn't a screamer. Dead wrong.

The sound tore through her throat and then echoed in her head, but she kept bending her knee and tugging.

"A little farther." His voice was level, somehow penetrating this fog of agony. She tried to focus on the warmth of his hand and the steadiness in his voice, but the pain was more than she could endure. Then she was moving and a layer of dust covered her face. Addison had a hold of her, dragging her, but there was pain.

So much pain.

When the world finally slipped away, taking her agony with it, the last sounds she heard was the distant barking of dogs.

Either canines were welcoming her to heaven, or help was on the way.

ALL IN

"**G**ood dogs." Addison knelt on the carpet in his study as he scrubbed both hands along Zeus, who ducked his head and leaned into the rubdown. Hera stood by, gazing at him in adoration, her tail wagging back and forth in excitement.

"They took up quite a ruckus." Collette's brother tugged at his cravat. He looked as worried as Addison felt—only without the dust and dirt in his hair and on his face. "Thank God."

"I sent them back. One time I'm happy as hell they disobeyed."

It was Rowan who'd realized something was wrong. Because when the dogs had returned home, they'd persisted in barking until the humans realized something was amiss. Addison didn't know how they'd known, but they had.

And just in time.

A shudder ran through him.

Most of the structure had collapsed behind them just before he'd glimpsed freedom. If he hadn't gotten them out of that room—if help hadn't arrived at that precise moment that it did—Addison ran a hand down his face. They wouldn't have survived.

If he could have walked out of there, he could have carried her. Having to crawl, he'd had to be more creative. But he'd been driven. Not knowing the extent of her injuries, he would have gone to hell and back if necessary to save her.

He very nearly had.

With the return of his canine friends and the arrival of both of their brothers and then several of his manservants, Addison had never felt more relief in his life. Rowan had added supports while Chaswick and one of the manservants pulled them free.

And when she came to once they made it into the open air, managing a weak laugh, he'd nearly cried.

But she wasn't out of the woods yet. Black rimmed his vision at the memory of her poor little foot.

He would be with her now if Lady Chaswick hadn't ordered him away.

Chaswick paced across the room for the hundredth time and Addison would have been pacing too if he wasn't so bloody exhausted.

Every inch of his body ached from moving planks and bricks. Recalling how his mother had demanded the doctor look at him first, his disgust with her threatened to return. He would have banished her from his life, put her on a carriage for one of his distant estates, but he had Fiona to consider. So instead, he'd ordered her to her chamber and she'd saved herself by going without argument. Had she finally realized that she'd pushed too far?

His mother had hurt the love of his life, and then he had nearly gotten her killed.

He'd spend his life trying to make it up to her. She would be happy.

They both would.

"Your Grace, my lord." The doctor appeared in the open doorway, a black leather bag at his side. "Although several muscles are strained, a few possibly torn, I don't believe her foot is broken. But I've ordered her to stay off of it for at least eight weeks. If she follows my instructions, she'll have a full recovery."

"And the rest of her?" Addison had to be sure she hadn't been injured anywhere else. "A few planks fell on us while I was bringing her out. I'm fairly certain I was able to cover her, but I need to be sure..."

The memory summoned black around the edge of his vision.

He hadn't cared about his pain, but there had been moments when the weight had nearly been too much for him.

"Aside from a few bruises, your fiancée shows no signs of any other injury." The doctor's brows furrowed in concern.

"Bedwell, you need to be checked out." Chaswick, who looked lighter already with the physician's report, stared at him in reproval.

"I'm fine."

"If you would, Your Grace, allow me just a moment, I can be quick with my examination."

"But I need to go to her—"

"You'll be no good to her if you're dead," Chaswick said. And at Addison's look of disgust, her brother added. "Allow the doctor ten minutes. She'll murder me if she discovers I didn't insist you have your injuries treated."

"Miss Jones is resting now. I've given her a tincture for the pain," the doctor added.

Addison wanted nothing more than to assure himself she was all right—to hold her. But at the same time, his body protested with every movement he made.

And Chaswick had a point.

It would behoove him to live, especially seeing as he fully intended to marry her tomorrow.

"Ten minutes," he conceded.

The doctor stepped into the room and placed his bag on one of the small tables. "Let's take a look."

Addison raised his hands to remove his jacket, only then remembering he'd wrapped it around Collette. Which had been a blessing. She'd had some protection while he dragged her through the debris. When his fingers fumbled at the buttons on his waistcoat, he glanced down.

Dried blood mingled with a few open cuts.

Chaswick noticed at the same time and crossed to the bell pull in the corner of the room. When a servant appeared not ten seconds later, the baron helpfully ordered hot water and towels.

"I'm always wary of infection," the doctor explained as he assisted Addison out of his vest. By the time Addison had the tails out of his shirt, and managed to get it over his head, his arms nearly gave out.

"Good God," Chaswick's expletive had Addison glancing down. Cuts and abrasions all but covered his chest. He imagined he had some colorful bruises on his back as well.

"You're lucky to be alive. And Collette..." The baron's voice caught. "I'm forever in your debt for getting her out."

"We wouldn't have made it if you and my brother hadn't arrived just in time." Addison scrubbed one hand down his face. "She wouldn't' have been in there if not for my stupidity."

"Mother of God." Rowan announced his arrival from the door with an expletive of his own. "I will kill whoever caused the collapse."

His brother's black eyes looked cold and hard.

"Vandals." Addison barely had the strength to speak, standing there as the doctor's hands probed along his back.

"I realize most of this is going to be somewhat painful but tell me if anything hurts worse than the rest."

"Umph." Addison grunted. All of it hurt. But he would heal. He was going to be fine.

"This went beyond vandalism. Three of the main supports were sawed through. It was criminal, and trust me, they will hang for this." Rowan wasn't one to exaggerate.

"I'm sorry, Row," Addison managed.

"It wasn't your fault." His older brother insisted.

And yet, somehow, Addison felt that it was.

"No, I'm sorry for all of this. For this nightmare of an evening. I was a fool to think mother would be fair—to think she'd ever see people the way I do." Addison turned to Chaswick. "I hope you'll accept my apologies for the way you and your wife were treated tonight. It won't happen again."

"You are thinking to send the duchess up north?" Rowan was watching him, one brow raised, reading his mind.

Along with the dukedom, Addison had also inherited the marquessate St. Alastair, which came with a decent-sized estate off the Loch Ryan.

"Perhaps her sister will be willing to reside with her

there." His Aunt Irene wasn't much different from his mother.

"But not Fiona."

"No." For the first time, he was happy his sister had decided to go to the school.

And although a part of him was saddened by the idea of sending his mother so far away, he refused to subject Collette to her venom.

Addison flinched at a particularly painful prod. "Bloody hell."

"Cracked ribs, Your Grace," the doctor announced. "You'll need to rest as well."

Rowan stepped deeper into the room to allow Addison's valet, who was carrying a robe, to enter. "A hot bath is being prepared." Mr. Brown frowned when his eyes flicked over Addison's condition.

Addison brushed the doctor away, snagged the robe from Brown, and summoned his last morsels of strength.

"After I've seen my fiancée." He shot a glance across the room to Chaswick. "Tomorrow I'll be obtaining a special license."

The baron's brows rose, and for a moment, he seemed to be weighing the meaning of Addison's declaration. But then he nodded as though comprehending what the others in the room did not.

"In that case, don't take too long having those wounds attended to." Chaswick said.

Addison dipped his chin in agreement and then turned to the doctor. "Mr. Brown will show you to my chambers. I'll meet you there shortly."

"Of course, my lord." The doctor nodded.

"This way, sir." Mr. Brown gestured for the physician to follow him.

Addison didn't wait to hear anymore. Oblivious to everything but his desire to be at her side, he made his way upstairs to find Collette.

~

SHE WAS NO LONGER TRAPPED under that small cot. Her eyes were heavy, her foot throbbed and her body ached, but she was alive.

Addison had saved them.

Being practically entombed beneath the debris like that had been terrifying for her; it would have been terrifying for anyone. It had to have gone beyond his worst nightmare.

But he hadn't panicked. Rather than being crushed beneath the weight of his fears, he'd found the wherewithal to free her foot.

And then gotten both of them to safety.

Vague memories of fighting for consciousness, knowing she was a burden to him, niggled at her. He could have left her there and gone for help. He could have escaped the nightmare without her. She would have understood. It would have been terrifying, but she would not have blamed him.

He'd refused to leave her.

The door creaked open, and she knew it was him before she even opened her eyes. Was that because he possessed her heart?

Or because she possessed his?

"Collette?" The slow rumble of his voice reached across the room.

"Addison." She fought off the heaviness of her eyes so she could look at him. Even in the soft glow of a few tapers, a light of love burned in his eyes.

Halting halfway inside, he stared at her. "I'm so sorry."

"Sorry?" His apology had her pushing herself up to sit. "For what?" Had he changed his mind about wanting to marry her? It would be ironic now that she saw their future differently.

"For my mother, for putting you in danger, for almost getting you killed."

"Oh, Addison, no." She reached out to him. "My love."

Overflowing tenderness washed through her when she noticed the cuts and scrapes on his hand.

"I never should have walked out of your mother's dinner. It was my fault. You simply followed me." How many times had he followed her one way or another? She'd been a fool not to realize the depths of character in this man before tonight.

"You made love to me," she added.

And it had been wonderful. Before the sky fell in. Before they'd both nearly been killed.

He lowered himself onto the mattress beside her, one corner of his mouth tilted up. "For the record, I am not sorry for that."

"Neither am I." She covered his hand with her other. "Not at all." Which was something of an understatement. "You didn't panic. You didn't leave me. You… saved us. How did you do it?"

He shuddered. But then he shook his head, staring at their hands.

"All that mattered was you… saving you… getting you out of there."

Tears welled in her eyes. *"All that mattered was you."*

Me.

"I'll never be able to thank you enough."

"You never have to thank me." He jerked his gaze back up to hold hers. "Just love me. Marry me. Be the mother of my children." Hope and pain flickered in his expression. *"Be my duchess."*

"Yes."

"Yes?"

"To everything." She no longer had even a single reservation. "Yes, to loving you, yes to marrying you, to children. Yes—to everything. You... overcame your fears—for me. I was going to allow fear to decide my future, our future. But not anymore. I want to be a duchess, not just any duchess, but *your* duchess. And if it takes the rest of my life, I want..." The strangest sensation crept over her.

"What do you want, love?"

"I want to be a most excellent duchess." She smiled at him, feeling incredulous. Would he laugh at that?

Of course, he would not.

"I will make mistakes," she quickly added. "Possibly many, in the beginning. And I'll likely get frustrated. But as long as you're my duke, I'm honored to be your duchess."

He raised her hands to his mouth, pressing a kiss to her fingers. "There is only one thing that would make me happier right now."

Collette hadn't ever imagined him quite like this—a full smile tilting his lips and his eyes so clear it was as though she could look right into his heart. Very deliberately, he pulled her into his arms, wincing slightly as he did so.

"You're hurt. You should be the one in this bed."

He slid her a glance that was far from proper. "As I was

saying… there is but one thing that would make me happier right now.

"A kiss?"

"I'll settle for that if you will."

And very gingerly, he dipped his mouth to meet hers.

EPILOGUE

*

"*T*he Duchess of Bedwell with her son, the duke, to see Miss Jones." Mr. Ingles announced. "Shall I see them in?"

Chase sent Collette a questioning glance. In the four days that had followed the accident, Addison had visited her at Byrd House four times. And they were lucky in that it was Bethany who volunteered to act as chaperone.

They were lucky, in that Collette's brother's wife often managed to find distractions that required she leave them alone for several minutes at a time.

Chase, Collette surmised, might not be so lenient. She couldn't help but feel the occasional twinge of sympathy for his future daughters.

"Are you quite certain you're up to seeing her?" Bethany asked from where she sat across the withdrawing room on the settee beside Chase.

Collette nodded.

Addison had said he would send his mother away—to Scotland, no less, where he owned a perfectly suitable, if not cold and drafty, castle. He'd said he refused to subject the woman he loved, the woman who would be the mother of his children and his future duchess, to his mother's insults.

Although Collette found the idea of his mother going to Scotland instead of herself somewhat ironic, she didn't want Addison to have to choose between his wife and his mother—not unless it was absolutely necessary.

Collette was willing to give his mother a second chance.

For Addison's sake but also for Lady Fiona's.

"Show them in, please." Collette answered her brother and sister-in-law's question by speaking to the butler directly, who nodded and then disappeared.

In the silence that followed his departure, Collette wiggled on the small settee where Chase had placed her not ten minutes earlier. Already, she was feeling antsy with her foot propped on the ottoman in front of her.

Aside from the pain of her very swollen and bruised foot, she was perfectly fine and yet she'd been ordered to keep off of it for eight weeks.

Two months!

Addison had taken pity on her the day before and carried her outside to sit in the garden for all of thirty minutes. When she'd protested that he too, was injured, he'd lifted her off the bed anyway.

"Not so injured I won't take advantage of every opportunity to have you in my arms."

Blasted man.

She'd taken full advantage of that time as well by inhaling his scent and placing delicate kisses along the line of his jaw.

As with each of his visits, her time with him flew by.

Mr. Ingles appeared in the open door, Addison behind him, and Collette's heart made a tiny skip of joy.

Because the second she met his gaze, all of her concerns, including but not limited to the dull throbbing in her foot and the stern-looking woman at his side, shrunk into nothing more than small annoyances.

Love, she decided, was an all-encompassing emotion that changed not only her heart but the way she viewed the world.

"Collette." He stepped aside for the duchess to precede him into the room. "My lord, my lady. You remember my mother?"

Chase was on his feet, as was Bethany, who dipped into a stingy curtsey beside Chase's quick bow. "Your Grace."

"Forgive me for not rising," Collette offered.

"But of course." The duchess's gaze flicked to Collette's foot, and Collette was glad of the sock and blanket that covered it.

Because it was not a pretty sight at all.

Addison, of course, had told her it was the most beautiful sight in the world. Beautiful because it would heal. The day before, in one of those fortuitous gaps of time when Bethany had excused herself, he'd admitted that he'd feared she could lose it. And then he'd pulled back the light blanket and placed a chaste kiss on her large toe.

He had to love her to do that.

"Won't you sit down? Mr. Ingles, if you'd be so kind as to have tea brought up?" Bethany returned to her seat, where she sat as primly and properly as any earl's daughter would.

The duchess lowered herself into one of the single high-backed chairs in the room and Addison took the space beside Collette.

"How are you feeling today, my love?" Addison stared into her eyes managing to convey all of his concern and affection while also maintaining his dignified ducal persona.

"I'm very happy to have escaped my chambers." She clasped her fingers around his, where he'd taken hold of her hand in the folds of her skirt. "And very happy to have visitors." She glanced toward the door. "You did not bring Zeus and Hera with you? I'm quite looking forward to thanking them properly."

"Tomorrow, I promise." Addison squeezed her hand. "But for today, Mother wishes a word with you."

The last time Collette had been in the duchess' company, she'd been the object of her disgust and resentment. But it was odd, in light of everything that had ensued since then, she couldn't summon much ill-will today.

Because the duchess was, in fact, Addison's mother. How could she not be grateful to her for bringing Addison into this world?

"I treated you and your family poorly, Miss Jones." The woman lifted her chin and leveled her stare on Collette.

This, Collette realized, was how a duchess said she was sorry. Was there any sincerity in the apology? Did she suffer even an ounce of remorse?

"Why?" Collette asked simply. Not because she wanted her future mother-in-law to grovel but because it was important they cleared the air in order to move forward.

As a family.

Chase, she realized, was watching her and looking...

Proud.

"I do not approve of you." The duchess' words had Addison stiffening beside Collette. His mother was quick to go on. "Hundreds, thousands of women all over England would go to great lengths to marry a duke, especially one so young and handsome as my son. I did not trust you. You are not only lowborn but also illegitimate. You've no training, no proper breeding. I would have much preferred Bedwell marry practically anyone but you."

"That's enough." Addison went to stand but Collette tugged at him to remain seated beside her.

"I initially refused his offer," Collette said. "For those same reasons. And yet here we are."

The duchess dipped her chin in agreement and a sense of understanding passed between the two of them.

"My son loves you."

"And I love him."

The duchess grimaced. "And so you and I shall come to terms with one another." Even while frowning, the duchess was a beautiful woman.

As far as apologies went, it was a rather weak one.

"And...?" Addison prompted from beside Collette.

It was Collette who stiffened this time.

"And, I look forward to helping you plan your wedding. St. George's, I think, will be quite lovely this spring."

Collette could not help but smile as she felt Addison shaking his head in what she already knew was his displeasure.

"I've had a special license in my pocket for three days now." He'd brought it out the day after the accident, wanting to slip her away to the nearest church. The doctor, however, had insisted she do nothing but rest and keep her foot elevated for at least a week before putting any strain whatsoever on the healing muscles.

They had canceled the wedding they'd already scheduled, and Collette hadn't complained. In fact, she'd been relieved at the idea of a private ceremony.

She had no wish to hobble down a long aisle, looking clumsy and weak as she made her way towards her groom. She hated even more the idea of being carried to the altar.

"Of which I must advise against making use of." Addison's mother pinched her lips and then turned to Bethany. "Don't you think, Lady Chaswick, that it's best for both of them, certainly for Miss Jones, if they take their vows with the requisite pomp and circumstance?"

"I cannot argue with that." Ironically, it was her brother who answered.

Collette shot him an accusing stare. What was he doing? Whose side was he on, anyhow?

"We're not waiting until spring," Addison stated.

Collette nodded, in perfect agreement with her fiancé.

They had lain together. And if that wasn't reason enough to hasten their wedding, she wanted to lie with him again. Not doing just that was considerably...

Frustrating. Even sitting beside him now, she wanted nothing more than to scoot closer, and run her hands up his sturdy thigh and—

"You'll be able to walk by the holidays. What about a Christmas wedding? At Easter Park." Bethany's suggestion broke into her thoughts.

Collette lifted the fan at her side and waved it, feeling unusually heated.

Christmas was nearly ten weeks away. Ten weeks!

"If you have a Christmas wedding, Lady Fiona can be present to witness your nuptials." The duchess seemed quite open to this compromise.

Chase met her gaze. "You could invite a few of the

friends you made at Miss Primm's, as well." His eyes twinkled. Because of course he was insinuating that she'd want to show them all that she'd not been broken by her dismissal.

"No doubt they'd be honored to attend." Bethany was to be no help either. "For a former teacher to wed a duke? A feather in the school's cap all around, I imagine." She winked.

Oh, but this was not fair at all. Because they all made excellent points. Not that she would wish to invite her former colleagues in order to make a show of her marriage to Addison, but because she had genuinely liked some of them.

"We can invite Miss Primm, Miss Shipley, and Miss Fortune—and didn't one of the other teachers write to you?" Bethany asked.

"Miss Priscilla." One of the teachers Collette had barely had a chance to get to know had written to express how sorry she was that Collette had had to leave and that she'd objected to the decision.

"And Diana and the marquess will have returned from their wedding journey by then as well. With the ceremony at Easter Park, your mother won't have to travel. What would you say to hosting a house party? Will you be up to that, Bethany?" Chase looked to his wife.

"I think that would be wonderful."

Collette studied her brother with great affection, thinking how much it would mean to have both of her sisters present for her wedding. All sets of eyes watched her, seemingly waiting for her decision. Even Addison was leaving this up to her.

Ten weeks until Addison could make love to her again,

though? Ten weeks until she could wake up beside him every morning?

Ten weeks of more wedding plans and being chaperoned and being dependent on her brother...

But having all of her family there... And if it meant getting off to a better start with his mother...

"I suppose a Christmas wedding would be nice."

Addison groaned and Chase burst out laughing. "Christmas it is then!"

With that decision in place, Bethany and Chase offered to show Addison's mother the garden and discuss more wedding plans, allowing Collette a few moments alone with Addison. It was a ruse, Collette knew, and she was coming to appreciate her sister-in-law more with each passing day.

No sooner had the door closed behind them when Addison lifted her carefully onto his lap and nuzzled the side of her neck.

"Ten weeks?" He sounded as disgruntled about it as she did. "Do you wish to torture me?"

"I know." Collette moaned softly, her skin practically on fire from the heat of his kisses. "A cruel punishment indeed."

"It doesn't have to be," he said. "There are ways..." His husky voice drew a shiver from her.

Collette smiled when she felt his hand drifting up her leg, beneath her skirts. "We'll have to be discreet." She gasped when his fingers grazed the tender flesh between her legs.

"No screaming." He warned.

"I'll be quiet," Collette whispered, her voice already shaking from need. "No screaming. I promise." But his fingers were touching her in the most glorious places and already she felt that delightful sharp feeling rising up. "Unless…"

Her body jolted and she arched herself into his touch. A little closer, a little more friction.

"Unless?" As though reading her mind, he gave her precisely what she needed.

"Unless a house falls on me, of course."

"I think we're safe in that regard," Addison laughed. "Unless, of course, you were speaking metaphorically."

"Ah…" Addison caught her cry with his mouth and proceeded to heighten her completion with his kiss.

"Figuratively speaking." Addison tucked her into his side afterward. "You can count on the house coming down many, many times over the next fifty or so years. Because like it or not, love, you're trapped with me forever."

Collette dragged her fingertips along the line of his jaw. In a beautiful sense of irony, spending her life with this man gifted her with incredible freedom. Freedom to love and be loved.

Joy burst in her heart and heat pricked the back of her eyes.

"Just so long as we're trapped together, Addison."

He nodded. "I wouldn't have it any other way."

BONUS EPILOGUE

"*I*'ve never danced this much in my life." Collette lowered herself onto the chaise beside her sister, who was now a marchioness, feeling exhausted but happy.

"That's because you spent most of the time hiding behind potted plants at the few balls you attended last spring," Diana teased but then added. "Sarah seemed to enjoy herself. That was good of you and Bethany to allow her to remain downstairs for the first few sets."

Their younger sister, who was three and ten now, had grown by leaps and bounds since moving to the country with their mother. No doubt Chase and Bethany would be wanting to bring her out before long. "Do you think she could ever have a season?"

Diana smiled. "If I can marry a marquess, and you can marry a duke, I've no doubt that despite her challenges, Sarah will take the *Ton* by storm."

"She's apt to marry a king." Collette laughed. Because her sister was correct in pointing out the irony of both of their present circumstances. Even now, she could hardly believe this elaborate party was being thrown to celebrate her wedding.

To *Addison.*

She searched the room until she found him laughing and talking with Lord Greystone, her brother, and a few other familiar looking lordly gents. And then a familiar thrill swept through her when he caught her eye and the corner of his mouth twitched in what she liked to think of as his secret smile.

For her.

With the wedding set to take place bright and early the following morning, their brother's country estate was near bursting at the seams with guests, but Collette had felt none of the squeeze. In fact, since Bethany had set aside one of the most elaborate chambers at Easter Park for Collette's use, she felt rather like a princess. Normally only ever opened up for visiting royalty, the state apartment, as Chase referred to the suite, was more luxurious and grander than anything she'd ever known.

She and Bedwell would share it for ten days, until after Christmas, when the two of them would journey to Brier Manor, rather than embark on a wedding journey.

His mother would be returning to London for what remained of the winter while the dower house was renovated to her liking, and once spring came around, Addison wanted to take Collette to the continent so they could have a real honeymoon.

"I cannot believe that you are just returned from Paris, and that you are married to Lord Greystone." Collette said.

Held up by inclement weather, Diana and her husband of less than a year had only just arrived at Easter House late the night before. What with the last-minute preparations for the ball that evening, the two sisters hadn't had a chance to do any real catching up.

Collette tilted her head and held her sister's gaze. "Are you happy?"

It was more of a statement than a question, really. Diana had always been vibrant, but there was something different about her now. She positively glowed.

"I cannot begin to tell you how wonderful he is." She sighed. "Yes, I'm so very happy, Collette. And I'm even happier knowing you won't be spending the rest of your life locked up in a stuffy school."

Before meeting Addison, Collette had been adamant that she would never marry. She'd insisted that she only wanted to teach. "It was a lovely school," she defended the place of her former employment.

Diana turned to stare across the room where Miss Primm, Miss Shipley, and a few of the other teachers hovered near the wall with the mothers and chaperones. "I suppose," she said. "That *is* where you found your duke."

"It had to have been fate." Collette almost whispered. Because if she hadn't wanted to teach, she never would have met Addison. And if she hadn't been sacked, he would not have found her in London.

"Do you love him?" Diana asked.

"More than anything." Collette answered from her heart.

"I think you are going to enjoy marriage then." Diana turned around to face her. "Has mother had her little talk with you? Or Bethany? Because I'm more than happy to answer any questions you might have about... relations." Diana didn't even have the shame to blush. "Trust me, you haven't anything to be concerned about."

Collette held back a grin and stared down at the toes of her silk slippers, which were peeking out from beneath the eggshell blue silk of her skirt.

"I'm quite informed." She bit her lip. Diana had been the first of the two of them to be kissed by a gentleman and was naturally less inhibited than Collette had ever been. Before Diana had married and gone away with her handsome marquess, the two girls had shared all of their secrets with one another.

Even the salacious ones—all of which had been Diana's. Collette smoothed her skirt.

"So, you aren't nervous about tomorrow?" Flickering lights from the candles in the chandeliers danced in Diana's narrowed gaze.

"Well, of course, I'm nervous to walk down the aisle with all the guests watching. And I'm nervous I'll do something foolish, like say the wrong thing during the ceremony. But I'm not nervous about marrying Bedwell." Collette lowered her voice. "And I'm not nervous about the wedding night."

Diana's brows shot up. "Have you and the duke--?"

"Hush." Collette felt herself blushing. "You mustn't say it out loud,"

But there was no chance that her sister would leave it at that. "When?"

"The night I was injured. Before Mr. Stewart's house collapsed."

Diana was shaking her head. "Such a nasty business. I do hope they catch the culprits who did that."

"As do I." Even two months later, Collette marveled that Addison had been the one to keep her calm throughout their ordeal. She hated to imagine what he'd gone through after she'd lost consciousness.

"And since then?" Diana pressed.

"Not with my injury," Collette stared down at her foot, which, aside from some lingering weakness, was good as new. "And Chase and Bethany have been relentless."

Diana leaned forward. "Isn't it marvelous?"

"Isn't what marvelous?" Lord Greystone's voice had Collette jumping. He and Addison had both managed to appear with neither Collette nor Diana noticing.

Which was saying something, considering that they were quite possibly the most handsome gentlemen in the attendance that night—Greystone wearing his usual flamboyant colors and Addison looking quite top-lofty and rather *dukish*, his light brown hair and silvery eyes contrasting with the jet black of his coat and breeches.

For a moment, the memory of the day he stepped into her classroom came to mind. He'd seemed terribly *dukish* then—a particularly endearing quality that she'd come to love almost as much as she loved his less dignified self.

Because the unshakeable confidence he showed most of the time made her all the more appreciative of the moments they were alone—those moments when he played with his dogs, or asked her opinion of one of his books, or sent her a wicked smile.

Those moments when he was simply Addison.

"All the perks that come with marriage," Diana smirked as she answered her husband. And then taking his hand, *her ladyship* rose to allow him to escort her onto the dance floor.

Left alone for the first time all evening, Addison bowed over Collette's hand. Glancing up to meet her gaze, he cocked one brow.

"My dance, I believe."

It was to be her last dance of the evening. Afterward, Collette would retire upstairs for the night, and the next time she saw him she'd be walking up the aisle of the village church to say her vows.

"Finally," Collette rose. They'd danced a country reel together earlier, but this was to be their first waltz. She'd looked forward to it all night.

Although Diana was the dancer amongst them, Collette had begun practicing for this moment as soon as her ankle had allowed her to do so.

Because while she was certain she'd stumble at times as his duchess, she refused to do so publicly at her pre-wedding ball.

Addison led her to the center of the floor where they took up their positions.

"How is it that I'm the luckiest man in all of England?" he whispered near her ear just as the music began. "Aside from the torture I've been put through these past few months."

"One more day," Collette tilted her head so she could gaze up at him. "I wish you could kiss me now."

Dancing with him was easier than she'd imagined. She should have known it would be, since she was beginning to believe they'd been made for one another.

Fate.

"Always with the kissing," he teased. But his gaze flicked to her mouth. He wanted the same.

And with that knowledge, a bolt of longing shot through her. One more day.

One more night.

After tomorrow, no one could prevent them from being together.

"I do hope your family isn't expecting to see much of us for the next few days. I fully intend to keep you locked in our bedchamber for no less than seventy-two hours after our nuptials. We have a good deal of time to make up for."

Collette grinned. "You don't wish to join the other gentlemen for the hunt?"

"I'll be saving my strength for more satisfying exertions." His eyes twinkled.

"What of cards in the gaming room?"

"I've already won the greatest prize."

"Very well. I suppose if I'm to be trapped—" she pretended to sigh even though the desire in his voice weakened her knees "—I might as well be trapped with a duke."

"Not with just any duke, madam, but with me," Addison added before sending her on a spin.

"My duke," she smiled up at him breathlessly. She was daunted but unafraid of all that the future held for the two of them. Because there would be many challenges to face, but she wouldn't be facing them alone. "I'll be happily trapped with my very own duke."

"And I," Addison said, dipping his mouth to brush the corner of hers. "Will be happily trapped with my duchess."

—The End—

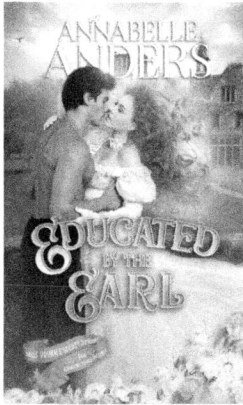

Preorder Miss Shipley's story, **EDUCATED BY THE EARL,** which is the next book in MISS PRIMM'S SECRET SCHOOL FOR BUDDING BLUESTOCKINGS. It releases Nov. 16th, 2021

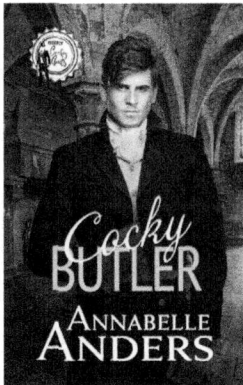

You can read Blackheart's story now! **COCKY BUTLER**

MISS PRIMM'S SECRET SCHOOL FOR BUDDING BLUESTOCKINGS

A NEW ANNABELLE ANDERS SERIES

TRAPPED WITH THE DUKE

Miss Colette Jones

EDUCATED BY THE EARL

Miss Victoria Shipley

PRETENDING TO BE A DEBUTANTE

Lady Priscilla

RESCUED BY THE RAKE

Miss Chloe Fortune

04-19-2022

ADVISING THE VISCOUNT

Miss Addy

07-12-2022

MAKE BELIEVE WITH THE MARQUESS

09-27-2022

SCHOOLED BY THE BASTARD

Miss Primm

January 2023

REGENCY COCKY GENTS

A NEW ANNABELLE ANDERS SERIES

Cocky Earl

Jules and Charley

Cocky Baron

Chase and Bethany

Cocky Mister

Stone and Tabetha

Cocky Brother

Peter Spencer's Story

Cocky Viscount

Mantis and Felicity

Cocky Marquess

Greystone's Story

Cocky Butler

September 14, 2021

Blackheart's Story

ABOUT THE AUTHOR

Married to the same man for over 25 years, I am a mother to three children and two Miniature Wiener dogs.

After owning a business and experiencing considerable success, my husband and I got caught in the financial crisis and lost everything in 2008; our business, our home, even our car.

At this point, I put my B.A. in Poly Sci to use and took work as a waitress and bartender (Insert irony). Unwilling to give up on a professional life, I simultaneously went back to college and obtained a degree in EnergyManagement.

And then the energy market dropped off.

And then my dog died.

I can only be grateful for this series of unfortunate events, for, with nothing to lose and completely demoralized, I sat down and began to write the romance novels which had until then, existed only my imagination. After publishing over twenty novels now, with one having been nominated for RWA's Distinguished ™RITA Award in 2019, I am happy to tell you that I have finally found my place in life.

Thank you so much for being a part of my journey!

To find out more about my books, and also to download a free novella, get all the info at my website!

www.annabelleanders.com

GET A FREE BOOK

Sign up for the news letter and download a book from Annabelle,

For **FREE!**

Sign up at **www.annabelleanders.com**

I love keeping in touch with readers and would be thrilled to hear from you! Join or follow me at any (or all!) of the social media links below!

Bookbub

Website

Goodreads

Facebook Author Page

Facebook Reader Group: A Regency House Party

Printed in Great Britain
by Amazon

26915218R00138